Counting Stars

by

Anne E Thompson

Published by The Cobweb Press through KDP
www.thecobwebpress.com
thecobwebpress@gmail.com

ISBN 978-0-9954632-1-9

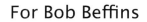

For Bob Beffins

Chapter One

The Door

They wouldn't know her, because they had never met. But that didn't matter. What mattered was that she remembered. It was what she did - remembered. It was why she was useful.

The guest house had three stories. She knew this, just as she knew they were connected by both the wide main stairs and the narrow hidden steps originally used by the servants. She chose the wide stairs, her hand skimming the smooth oak bannister as she climbed.

She wanted the third floor. The first two floors were the regular rooms, often used by families who booked two or three of them at a time. There were standard doubles, large twin-bed and tiny single rooms. Each one boasted a sink, but the guests had to leave the safety of their room if they needed the bathroom. There was a selection of bathrooms with over bath showers and single cubicle toilets placed conveniently along both floors.

But the third floor was special. The third floor was where the *en suite* rooms lived. Each room had a double bed, matching furnishings and a small private bathroom, for guests who could afford the *en suite* tax, who could afford a little luxury. They were at the top of the house (if one does not include the attics, which had been renovated for the staff to use) and they enjoyed a view of the sea. A tiny view. A glimpse really, between the tree tops.

However, it was not to one of these rooms she went. It was to the rather unnecessary extra bathroom. It sat between two rooms, tucked back in an alcove. The wood slatted door was painted to match the other doors and would have been easy to miss, angled as it was away from the landing, almost as if trying to hide. A shy door. But she knew it was there and cautiously opened it.

Inside was what one might expect to see in an upstairs convenience. Behind the door as you entered, on the left, was a white china toilet with high water closet and old fashioned chain for flushing. Opposite it, on your right as you entered, was a white sink. It had been tastefully littered with miniature soaps and scrubbed sea shells.

None of this interested her. It was as she remembered. She went straight to the cupboard. It was set in the wall to the left of the toilet, opposite the door, was raised a good four feet from the floor and reached nearly to the ceiling. The door was tongue and groove, painted white to match the chinaware. There was a small lock on the right, and she was relieved to see the key was still in it. They had always kept it there for fear it would be lost, some traditions never change. It seemed unlikely that a guest would bother to open the door even if they ventured in to use the toilet.

She reached up and turned the key. It was small and stiff but it ground its way round and the door swung open.

Inside there were no tidy piles of linen or spare toilet rolls. There were steps. Great stone steps which led up and away.

Smiling, she closed and locked the door, putting the key safely in her jeans' pocket. She could feel it there, digging into her hip. She would come back later with the family.

#

It was dark when she returned, and very late. She first woke the mother who seemed to be expecting her, even though she hadn't been told the plan. That had been considered too risky, too much of a security threat. So the mother had been directed there, following her escape from the hospital, but given no details.

They spoke little as they gathered some warm clothes, pushing them into a small backpack. Then they woke the children together, the mother going first into the room, hushing them, telling them it was an adventure, they needed to be quiet. She had worried they would speak in their high child voices, voices that seem to penetrate so clearly and wake someone. But they were older than she had expected, the boy almost as tall as his mother, at that lanky thin stage that so often precedes manhood. They seemed to catch the mood of the adults and, compliant with sleepiness, they allowed themselves to be hurried from their beds and guided up the stairs to the third floor.

She could tell the mother was surprised to be taken into the small washroom. She held her children close to her and watched silently as the door was locked, the key to the cupboard was produced. They all peered in, stared at the steps. Would the girl manage? The mother spoke a single word:

"Up?"

She nodded, understanding the question, knowing the answer.

And so they climbed. First onto the lowered lid of the toilet, using it as a first giant step, then into the cupboard. She went last, helping the mother, passing her the girl, helping the boy. She squeezed in behind them, twisting to pull the door shut, turning the key, delaying anyone who might follow. Then they went up and round.

The steps, which you might have assumed, as the mother did, would descend, first went up. The steps climbed steeply, turning as they went, following the line of the chimney breast. Then a straight section, long and thin with a slight draught that made the family shiver. The floor was different here, weathered floorboards, and they knew they were crossing a section of the attic, hidden from view behind the thick stone walls. Then at last, down. The steps were built into the ancient walls, unseen, long forgotten by all but a few.

It was very narrow. The boy caught his elbow on the rough stone wall and cried out, angry with the wall, angry with himself. His sister's eyes grew very large as red blood oozed from the cut, and they wondered if she might cry. The mother touched her hair, comforting and warning in one smooth stroke; her eyes telling the boy to be brave, he was a man now. They continued, down, down. The girl almost jumping, the steps were so tall, clinging onto the back of her mother for support. Down, down. Below the second floor, then the first, then the ground. Into the earth.

The steps finished and they faced a tunnel. Long and dark. A passage with no end. Where monsters might live. She snapped on a torch and the monsters retreated, back into the gloom beyond the beam. They walked on.

The floor was earth, hard and dry. Then stones, then rock, carved by men long ago, deep under the ground. The rock was shiny in places, she worried they might slip and they all took a hand, turning slightly to walk in pairs along the narrow tunnel. On and on where once they had walked down. Not stopping, not speaking, though she knew they could now. For they were under the sea and no one would hear but fish and crabs. But what would they say? Would the mother ask about the hospital, with the harsh lights and probing questions? Or the children ask about their father, ask why he had been taken? Would they worry about spy drones, ask whether they were violating some law set by the Global Council? No, words would only stir emotions and they needed to

4

be locked away until there was room to set them free. Later, much later.

The girl started to slow, for the walk was a long one. She thought of her bed, of the dreams she had left, and began to whine, to make tiny whimpering sounds. The boy was silent, just looked at her, his eyes unreadable.

Still they went on. The air was stale and chill but they were moving and not cold. It smelled of sea and salt and mermaid hair. Still holding hands, almost dragging now, wondering if they could make it, wondering how long to go, how far to return.

Finally, they arrived. The passage widened, began to slope upwards, then four rough steps hewn from the rock and then sand, soft and damp, clinging to their shoes, creeping into their socks. They came up, out of a cave and she saw they had arrived. The sky was black and starless when she turned off the torch. Their faces were very white.

Still silent she turned. First she hugged the mother, pushing hope and strength into her. Then the girl, lightly and with affection. Then she hugged the boy, roughly, willing him to be brave, to take his father's place. Then she left them, turning swiftly away and dipping back into the cave. They were on their own now.

The Island

The mother led the children away from the cave. They were whimpering now, pleading to sit, to rest a while. Even the boy was making a fuss, his discomfort making him revert to childhood. But it was too cold. They needed to find shelter, if only for what remained of the night. The wind tugged at their clothes, pushing against their exposed faces, tangling their hair.

They stumbled over the large pebbles that filled the cave entrance and onto the hard sand. The mother could not tell if the tide was going in or out and wanted to get to higher ground. It was very dark, she wished she had a torch. They walked along the sand, over the debris left at the high tide mark and onto rough tufts of grass, the type you only find on dunes. It whispered in the wind and stretched out spiteful fronds to slice their skin. With an arm around their shoulders, she guided them onto what seemed to be a pathway, packed sand that wound through the grass. There were shrubs now, and it was warmer as the land dipped, away from the biting wind that drove from the sea.

They came to a track, hard packed mud and puddles. She didn't know if they were headed to safety or danger, but they would not survive outside, so she urged them onwards. The boy staggered into a dip, soaking his foot and crying out in tired despair. They were exhausted. The girl had grown silent, which was more worrying.

Just when she felt they could go no further and was looking for a hollow in which they could shelter, they came to a cottage. Unlit, even as they approached, so no automatic lighting, which was strange. It loomed, black and double fronted. Glaring at them. An Edgar Allan Poe house. There were no lights lit at all, the windows black holes that watched them. Driven by despair, she knocked on the wooden door, hammering with her fist. The girl jumped, the boy leant closer into her.

A light appeared in an upstairs window. Then sounds of movement. The lights followed the sound, appearing in windows as the movement passed through the house, coming lower, nearer. Then footsteps, and the door opened. Just a crack at first, to see who was there, then wider when the woman and children could be seen. They were hardly a threat.

The mother looked up at a man. He stood, holding the door, watching them, deciding. He wore an old fashioned sweater made of knitted wool, frayed at the edges, his wrists protruding, strong, thin, speckled with hair. Blue eyes appraised her below remarkable eyebrows. It was his eyebrows she noticed first. They were very black and sloped upwards, giving him the appearance of an owl, a great horned owl. She saw he wore no bar code and seemed very old. He saw their exhaustion, the despair in their eyes and he beckoned them inside.

"Come, it's warm in here. I'll light a fire."

They followed him, into a small room with chairs arranged around a hearth. A cosy room. A safe place. He motioned for them to sit and busied himself with the fire. He asked no questions. They struggled out of their coats, clutching them close as they sat on the chairs, feeling the relief in their legs. The room was bright, the light from the fire bouncing off the rosy cushions, the shining wood and the rugs that littered the carpet. It felt too hot after the bitterness of the wind, almost airless. Their bodies responded instantly, slowing their thoughts, relaxing their senses.

The door opened and a woman appeared, round faced, smiling, carrying mugs that steamed. Hot milk with flakes of chocolate, cinnamon to sprinkle on the surface. The boy picked up a spoon and began to scoop out the flakes, burning his tongue, not caring. The girl waited until the heavy mug was cool enough to lift, then holding it in both hands, took greedy sips, letting the warmth spread through her. The old couple watched the young family drink. The girl nestled close to her mother and was asleep almost instantly. The boy sat upright, wary, unsure, wanting to relax but afraid, feeling the need to protect his mother and sister but unsure how. He wished his father was there, he would know what to do. The mother was too tired to care. They had no choice, not now.

The old man stood and turned towards them. He asked their story.

The mother spoke in low tones, describing the steps, the tunnel, the beach. No more. She didn't know how much was safe to share.

The man looked at the old woman. Their eyes told a story. She gave an imperceptible nod. He took a chair next to the fire, stirred the embers, chose his words.

"I know the tunnel of which you speak. I know the house where it begins. I know the girl who guided you here. She is a rememberer. You are safe here, at least for now. We will find you beds. Tomorrow, you can tell me more of your story. But first, what are your names?"

"Names?" asked the mother, confused, fear beginning to grow. Was this a trap?

"Yes," said the man, "names. You must trust us now, let me know the gaps in your story."

The mother paused. She fingered her bar code, feeling the familiar hard plastic edges, wondering why this man, this stranger, needed more information than that.

"That's enough John," said the old woman, "Let them come upstairs, before they fall asleep in their chairs. Come my dear, let's find you what you need." She held out her hand, beckoning for them to follow. Her face was round and kind. One trusted a face like that.

They followed her up wooden stairs, their feet noisy on the steps. Smelling wood smoke and something sweet. The carpet on the landing was thick and pale, the mother worried they would leave a mark. She paused, struggling to remove their shoes. The old woman stopped her. It didn't matter. The mother nodded, wondered again where they were, wondered at this strange cottage that seemed to be lost in time.

They went into a room. A single bed ran along one wall under the sloping ceiling, a small table next to it under the window. The woman saw what was on the table and gasped. She sat on the bed, picked it up, turned the pages.

"I thought they had all been destroyed," she whispered.

8

"No dear, that is what they wanted you to think. You will find that there are many things which are not as they seem on the mainland. But tomorrow, we will talk tomorrow. You must help these precious ones to bed and get some rest."

The woman went to a cupboard, pulled out blankets and pillows, and snowy linen. She folded the blankets, one for each child to lie on, next to their mother on the rug. It would do for the night. She showed them the bathroom, gave them clean tee shirts, and left.

The mother made the children wash their hands and rinse their mouths. There was no dryer, only lengths of fluffy cotton hanging on a rack, so they rubbed themselves dry with them, hung them back. They were too tired for more. They did not want to wear the tee shirts, they looked like they might be vests that belonged to the old man, clean but foreign. She didn't make them, their clothes were dry. They stripped down to their underwear and slid beneath the covers. Almost instantly their eyes closed and their breathing settled. Then she washed, changed, lay down. There seemed to be no way to extinguish the light, so she reached at last for the lamp shaded in frills, found a manual button and let darkness enfold her.

She lay in that strange bed and listened to a strange whirring, loud and constant. When she slept she dreamed of giant bees, carrying her children away. During the night the girl left her bed on the floor and crawled in next to her, sharing her warmth and pressing her hard head against her shoulder.

#

In her dream, the bees swarmed, not letting them rest. There was screaming, louder and louder, she reached for her son as he tumbled through the sky. Her eyes snapped open.

The whirring outside continued, a deep hum. It was joined now by seagulls calling to each other. She moved her head. Light was flooding through the curtains and she could see her son, lying curled on the floor, a sleeping lump. Her daughter wriggled next to her, changing position but not waking. Her arm ached under the heavy weight and she slowly extracted it, slowly, slowly, willing the girl to sleep on. When it was free the blood painfully fizzed and popped back into place. She wanted to stand, to look out of the window, to read the book, to use the toilet, but she did not want to wake her children. So she waited, letting her mind wander into those places she kept locked. Thinking of her husband, wondering where he was, if he lived, if he would still know her, know the children, know himself. A tear slid the length of her cheek and sat, tickling her ear. She closed her eyes and remembered.

#

When the children woke, she swung out of bed and went to the window, seeking the source of the hum, loud, constant. She recognised it at once, had seen wind farms as a child. Thought it strange to find one here, the island must not be connected to the grid. She remembered the words of the old woman, wondered what else was not as she had been told.

They showered and dressed. Yesterday's clothes. She would need to find some spare clothes before long. Nothing she could do now, they had left without a plan, left when they could, while they could.

She stood and fiddled with her bar code, adjusting it slightly while the boy complained, wanting to go downstairs to find food. They were hungry now, food was all that mattered. How quickly their needs changed and became their sole concern. The bar code had caught on her hair and she struggled to free it. Looked at it with new eyes, thinking of the old man who did not use bar codes. Why not?

Everyone had a bar code. It told people everything they wanted to know, your line of work, your education, what you owned, your family situation. All the things you might wonder about a stranger were clearly marked, so you could evaluate a person in seconds, decide if they were worth speaking to, could be trusted. Different colours and shades and widths that represented the sum of a person. She had gone to London once, seen a man with a strip of green in his code so dark and wide, all could see that he owned great swathes of land. Her green was narrow and light, enough for one small house in a large town. A house she would probably never see again.

There was a strip of colours at the top. These changed annually, everyone was issued with an updated bar that reflected their current status, changing with promotions, childbirth, relationships. But the code below, a series of letters and numbers, stayed the same, was issued at birth. It reflected her age, the place she was born, the profession of her parents. Everyone had one. It made them all the same, meant no one could hide. Made it harder for criminals to escape. Criminals and people like her, people who were deemed different.

They were used for payment and to order goods, allowed you function in society. There had been campaigns, years ago, for the bar codes to be implanted or tattooed. But people had resisted the permanency of such an idea, had wanted them to be changeable, disliked the thought of something being incorporated into their physical self, something artificial. So now they were removable, easily worn, an integral part of life. Only someone with something to hide would neglect to wear one.

Her hair was free. She combed it with her fingers and allowed herself to be led down the stairs, acquiescing to their impatience.

They followed the smell of fried bacon and found the kitchen. The man and woman were both there, sipping coffee next to empty plates. Harmonious, content. The old woman got up when she saw them, set plates on the table, busied herself frying eggs, making drinks, cutting bread. The family concentrated on eating, glad to avoid having to speak, each lost in their thoughts.

The girl was wondering if they would be offered more hot chocolate, and would she have to wear the same clothes forever now they had left. She watched her mother, saw tired lines around her eyes and knew that she must not ask. She reached for another slice of bread, catching her brother's eye.

He was eating quickly, not sure if they could stay here beyond breakfast and not wanting to walk again. It had been too long, too cold. Then having to share a room with his sister. Alright for one night, but again? He was suspicious of these people, with their lack of bar codes and their house from a previous century. Why would people live like that? His mother was not speaking, not telling them anything. She had not told them anything for a long time now, nothing they wanted to know anyway. Not since the hospital.

His mother too was thinking about the hospital. Perhaps it was the sunlight, streaming brightly through the window. The hospital had been bright too, many bulbs shining, banishing dark places, unseen dirt, but also weather and time and space. One long continuum of light. Harsh and intolerant, striking their eyes as they waited, sinking into their worried heads and making them ache. A cruel light.

Everything was automated of course, screens that welcomed them, as if they had chosen to be there. Screens that spoke, guided them to the correct waiting room, told them where to sit, how long they should expect to wait. An age - they had waited an age, while she worried about what they would find, what they would say. The technology was faultless, but there were still not enough doctors, still too many people needing to be seen. Some were there by choice, coming to be healed of some malady, something too serious for the online medicare to deal with. Others were like her, summoned by email, needing to be checked.

Everyone in their waiting room was there by summons. She could tell that by the faces: worried expressions, red rimmed eyes, tight lips. The doctor, when he appeared, was no more than a boy, hardly old enough to be qualified. She guessed that experience counted for little in a world that demanded you keep up with the latest technology, could use the instruments effectively, follow procedure without question.

Questions, many many questions. They had repeated them over and over, recording her answers, analysing the results. They had already taken her husband, sent him for further 'treatment'. Now they must decide if she too were an unfit parent, needed to be removed from the children. She tried to be wise, to guess the evidence that would be gleaned from each answer but it had been too difficult, too many questions seemed innocuous, she could not guess which were the ones that mattered, which were the ones that would destroy her life.

It was after the first bout of questions, while she was awaiting further examination and had asked to use the washroom, that the nurse had approached her. Pretending to show her the way, though she understood the directions even if there weren't all the signs, the nurse insisting on accompanying her. Then, as she entered the cubicle, slipping her a scrap of paper, telling her she needed a holiday; before turning, blending back into the white anonymity of the hospital corridor. She looked at the paper when she was home, locked in her bathroom, trying to wash away the sterility of the hospital, the smell of cleaning fluids. It had been a scrap, torn from a medical form perhaps. It was the first handwritten note she had ever seen - what could need to be written that couldn't be typed, sent by email? It just contained an address. No explanation, just an address. The address of the guesthouse next to the sea.

She reached for her coffee. It was strong and bitter and brought her back to the present. She needed to ask how long they could stay, if there was a plan. To make decisions. To find clothes for herself and the children. To find out what this place was, who these people were. To decide what came next.

The children had finished eating. The boy was wriggling in his seat, sliding from side to side, like he used to when he was much younger. The old woman showed him where the bathroom was. The girl slid from her seat too, wanting to be free, asking if she could go outside, see the garden. The old man, John, said he would take both of them, asked her to join them when she had finished.

#

She found him in the garden, sitting with her daughter on a seat that rocked. He stood when she arrived and the boy pounced, happy to take his place, eager to see how high the swing could go, if he could make his sister squeal.

The mother and the old man walked to the edge of the garden to where an old stone wall separated from them the track. They looked towards the sea, hearing the waves, the gulls and the whirring from the wind farm. She touched her bar code, feeling the security of it. He looked strangely bare without one, almost indecent, as if he had something to hide. He followed her gaze and smiled, a smile that showed he understood, had seen it before, already knew her questions.

"You wonder why I don't wear one? If I am trying to hide who I am? If that means you shouldn't trust me? No, you can trust me. I believe you don't really have much choice actually." He smiled, taking the sting from his words. "Here, sit, I'll explain what I can." He sat on the low stone wall, gesturing for her to do the same.

She turned, her back towards the sea and rested on a rock. It wobbled and she hoped she would not spoil his wall. The sun warmed her face, searing through the wind that tugged at her hair.

"We don't have bar codes here because we don't need them," he began. "We only need to know what people want to tell us, and

14

we think there is more to a person than a set of numbers, a combination of strips of colours. You are more than what you own, your education, your family. That's why we reject them. They keep people small.

"I know what you've been told, that individuality is dangerous, that it leads to wars and greed and terror. Maybe it does in some cases. But it also keeps you human, lets you know that you are unique, created to be special. Don't let them take that away from you. You do have a right to privacy, to independence. You can make your own decisions, you don't have to fit their mould."

His voice was deep and smooth and he spoke slowly, calming her as much with his tone, though she thought his words were dangerous.

"People have always feared individuality," he went on. "We used to pretend that we didn't, used to say that we prized uniqueness. But we didn't really, we had many unwritten rules about how things should be done.

"In many ways the Global Council is simply writing what people have always said and done. Which is why it was so easy to implement back at the start, when they first took power. But that doesn't make it right."

He saw the doubt in her eyes, sought to explain.

"In the old days, if you look at our history, we prized artists, respected their individuality, thought that it was okay for them to be eccentric, to maybe wear unusual clothes and have long hair. Society could cope with that, because that was how an artist was *meant* to behave. But if a teacher, lawyer, politician - someone in authority, wore those same clothes, let his hair grow long, people would've been outraged. They would've tried to have him removed from his job, thought he wasn't professional.

"Do you see? Even in the old days, there were rules, codes of behaviour we expected everyone to stick to. They weren't written down. But the pack instinct has always been there. That's all this new Council are, they are allowing the pack instinct to dominate. Much of it is good, there are no more wars, terrorism is almost unheard of, the world has become fairer and safer. But they have overstepped the mark. That's why we do what we do.

"So, here we refuse to wear bar codes. It's a small thing but it helps us to feel unique again, special, human."

Unconsciously her fingers fiddled with her code, tracing the plastic while she thought about what he said. Not having a bar code would exclude her from shopping, ordering goods and transport, using online services. But perhaps they were unobtainable on the island anyway. She felt as if she had stepped into the pages of a history lesson.

He watched her, assessing.

"I am John, my wife is called Agnes. What is your name? Who are your children?"

"I'm Lena," she said, trying to trust him, to ignore those thoughts that told her he was clever, making her feel secure so that he could trick her. She knew her name told him something personal. Many people chose to use letters from their bar code for names, others used names selected by their parents. Names hinted at possible attitudes towards how individuals should be viewed in society.

The old man looked back to the children. The boy was alone on the swing now, flinging his legs back and forth in an effort to make it go higher. The girl was sitting on the ground, making a heap of small stones, lost in her own world. He hid his smile, it was as he had suspected, they were who he had assumed they were. He had been expecting them to come, though not yet. The watchers must have decided it was safer to move them quickly, before he and Agnes could be warned.

"And the children? Who are they?"

16

"Max," she told him, "my father was called Max. And Lucy. My husband is Den. But he's –"

She stopped. What could she say? She didn't know for sure where he was, if she would ever see him again, if he even existed in the form that she thought of him.

The old man patted her hand, guessing her thoughts. "We have some time," he told her, then stood and stretched, arching his back to chase away an ache from sitting against the hard rock. "I'll go and tell Agnes. Then we can make some plans, decide what is for the best."

He walked across the lawn, lifting his arm in salute as he passed the children. Lena watched him go. She stood and called to her children, to Max and Lucy.

Altered

Lena walked slowly to the kitchen. That conversation had not gone well at all. The children had announced that they wanted to keep their bar codes, like everyone else, and what would happen to them anyway now they had left? They didn't even have their computers, had left them in the guesthouse. How could they contact their friends, what about schooling? Why had she brought them here?

It was Max really, Lucy would have agreed to anything. He was only being difficult because he was tired and found new things disturbing, Lena knew this but it did nothing to make her own task easier. She wound her way back to the kitchen, past the vegetable patch and the neat flower beds, over the lawn and along the small stone path that curved under trees and led to the kitchen door.

Agnes was in the kitchen, chopping vegetables. She smiled when Lena walked in, so she picked up a knife and sat next to her. She watched as Agnes held the vegetables firmly with one hand on a wooden board, slicing quickly with the other. Lena had never cut vegetables before. She ordered all her meals, like everyone else, scheduling them all to arrive at set times throughout the week. She had a coded cold storage box next to the door and, if she happened to be out, the food was left there for her to collect when she got home. It arrived ready to microwave or reheat, unless she ordered ready-eat food, which arrived hot. That didn't happen very often, not on their budget.

"Do you want to help?" asked Agnes.

"Yes, but, not entirely sure I'll be much use," admitted Lena. "Cooking was never really a hobby."

"No, I was lucky, I learned to cook when I was young," said Agnes, resting her knife on the table. "Most people still did at least some cooking then, even if it was only for special occasions. Now people only really cook for fun, if that's what they enjoy doing.

"We don't get deliveries on the island, obviously. So since we've been here I've done it all. John grows most of the vegetables and we have some fishermen who will deliver orders for us, keep our stores topped up - tea, coffee, that sort of thing. I don't really enjoy it, but needs must. We don't use drones for deliveries.

"Here, why don't you peel these carrots? Like this, you just run the peeler along the edge. That's it." She moved the onions to a large pot and put a pile of carrots next to Lena, putting an old bowl below to catch the peelings.

"I never learned to sew though," she continued, pulling potatoes from a large sack, showering dirt on the tiled floor. They sat on the table, muddy and smelling of earth. Agnes began to slice off the peel, exposing their moist white insides.

"My Grandmother sewed a little, when she was young," explained Agnes, "but by the time I was born everyone bought all their clothes. It was a bit like cooking is now, a few people still sewed, for fun or to save money, but very few. It was so much easier to order them online or go to the shops.

"So, I'm afraid we'll have to order you and the children some clothes," she said, looking at Lena. "We can give a list to the next fisherman that stops here, ask him to send some. They won't mind. We never go to the mainland now, obviously."

"Do they know that you're here?" asked Lena, thinking that actually, it *wasn't* obvious, but not liking to say. She was not sure how much information she should ask for. Not sure how much she wanted.

"Oh yes, of course, you can't hide a whole island. They seem to have decided to leave us alone though, as long as we don't cause them any trouble. To be honest, I think they are relieved in a way, it solves a problem for them when the altering doesn't work. It doesn't sometimes you know. Not that they like to advertise that."

She pulled another potato from the bag. It was soft and smelly so she threw it in with the peelings and selected a new one.

"What do you mean?" asked Lena. She had stopped peeling and was staring at Agnes, not sure if she would cry or be sick. Or maybe this would be good news - so long since she had heard any of that.

Agnes looked up from the potato, paused, put it down and reached for Lena's hand.

"Oh, my poor girl. You don't have a clue, do you." She stood, brushing specks of dirt from her apron. "Let's have some tea and a proper chat. We need to sort out what's going to happen anyway, but maybe you need to understand a few things first. Information on the mainland is so very controlled. Are you feeling up to it?"

Lena nodded. Better to know, to stop guessing, wondering, being lost in a maze of confusion. You could prepare for what you knew, fight back if needed. Not knowing left you helpless, in a chasm.

Agnes filled the kettle and set it to boil. She pulled two china cups from the cupboard, added tea, sat back down.

"You know why you were sent to the hospital? What they were looking for?"

Lena nodded.

"You know about the alterations?"

"A little. Only what has been announced. And rumours, lots of rumours. I'm not really sure what's true." She felt nearer to tears now, not sure if she could have this conversation. She had spent so much energy not thinking, not letting herself consider possibilities. Was it really better to know?

Agnes stood and made the tea, put a steaming cup in front of Lena, sipped her own, ordered her thoughts, decided what to say.

"I'll start with a little history. Bear with me, you'll know some of it but maybe not all.

"Before the Global Council, before we got properly organised, if there was trouble of any kind: crime, terrorism, that sort of thing; society used to lock away the culprits. If you go back long enough of course, people were executed - they still were until quite recently in some countries; but in England that had finished a long long time ago. Obviously people who were a danger to society needed to be removed, but the only real option was to lock them in a secure place, a prison. Before my time, of course, but I heard talk of it when I was small.

"It didn't work terribly well, there was not the funding for them to be very nice places, people were sometimes crowded together more than they should have been, and people who had committed minor offences were sometimes put with more serious criminals. It also didn't work. Most people, when they were let out, continued to commit crimes."

Lena nodded, she knew all this, had heard it at school during history lessons. Had seen pictures of grim buildings that had served as prisons. She even knew someone who had toured a disused prison on the moors, during a holiday. A few were still preserved, a physical reminder of the past, museums. Especially those that had been in remote places, where the Council had decided to conserve the area, away from towns and cities.

Agnes swallowed her tea and continued.

"Now, a quick change of subject but it's related. Alongside all the other developments we've seen recently, is an understanding of how the brain works.

"Brain surgery always came far behind all the other medical disciplines you know. Long after surgeons were operating on hearts, kidneys, things like that, they did not even begin to look at the brain, it was considered too difficult. So, when they did finally start to open up the skull and examine what was inside, it took them a little while to properly master what they could do. They learnt which different parts of the brain did what pretty quickly, and began to do surgery when it was necessary; but the technology to actually alter what was inside, to change the way a person thinks, is fairly recent.

"Of course, once they worked out how to start altering what was happening in the brain, to start changing a person's reactions to things, the opportunities seemed boundless. The first thing they did was alter the way a criminal thinks. I don't understand it, you'll have to ask someone better educated than me, but they managed to change the way a person responds to certain things. They can basically take away a person's desire to commit certain crimes.

"In many ways this was good, took away the need for all those awful prisons. But of course, they couldn't always be sure what else might get altered. There have been a few sad cases, people being left with not much ability to decide anything. The part of the brain that controls decisions and desires is so close to the part that stores memory. Some people even lost the ability to speak, by the time they decided what they wanted to say, they forgot the beginning; they couldn't hold the words in their head for long

21

enough to say them. Though these mistakes are becoming rarer as the technology improves.

"The trouble is, who decides what needs to be altered? The Global Council have written some pretty strong guidelines but things get changed, individual countries' governments decide how to implement the new policies. That's where we've got to now; if someone is considered a threat to the peace of society, they get altered. We think that's what has happened to your husband."

She paused, waited for Lena to respond.

There, it had been said now. All those hidden worries had escaped, been let out in the real world. Lena breathed. She looked at the carrot lying forgotten on the table. She looked at the tea going cold in her hand. She heard the children, playing noisily outside, arguing about whose turn it was. The world was the same yet everything was different. She could not speak, did not trust her mouth to form words. So she nodded. She wanted Agnes to continue, needed to hear this, to know if there was any hope. Otherwise she might as well go back to the mainland, let them alter her. Maybe she would be happy that way.

"We were already living on the island when they changed who could be altered, when it became used not just for criminals, so we stayed. There are a few routes here, the one you used but mainly the fishermen drop people off. We usually know when people are coming so can welcome them properly. Most people only stay a few hours and then we get them on a boat, send them off to Asia."

"Asia?" Lena frowned. Why Asia? Was that any better?

"I think that's enough for now, why don't we talk again later?" said Agnes. It was not a suggestion. "Now, you write down the clothes sizes you need and we'll see if we can get some things for you. Your little family will be different to most of our guests, because of your husband. We need to find out if we can get him here, and that may take a few days, so you'll need to stay." She saw the shock in Lena's eyes as her words began to register.

"It may not be possible dear. We need to find out some information first, and that takes time. It won't be easy but you will need to wait and see. If there's anything that can be done, we will try. It may be too late.

"Now, I need to get this soup boiling and you need to spend some time settling those children. Why don't you take them for a walk around the island? Everyone is friendly," she paused, wanting to reassure,

"It's safe here, no need to be afraid of people here. Everyone is on your side now."

The Woman

It was during an afternoon that Lena saw her. She had taken the children to the beach, Max grumbling that it was boring and he wanted to go home where there was a computer; Lucy walking next to her, swinging her arm and humming.

They retraced their steps from the night they had arrived, along the lane to the dunes, and onto the beach. It was a long walk but there didn't seem to be any cars on the island, none she had seen anyway. There was a tractor type vehicle she had noticed, recharging in one of John's sheds, the bulky flex joining it to the socket on the wall. Lena wondered if the wind power was effective, wondered why the island chose to not be connected to the grid. Perhaps they valued their independence, though that was a dangerous ambition in today's world.

Walking was inconvenient, they weren't used to things not being immediate. If you wanted something or to go somewhere, they were accustomed to simply inputting that in their computers, solving the problem straight away. It had been so easy to text for a car, they arrived within minutes and took you to your destination, however far that might be. Very few people owned their own cars, just a few eccentric old men and the very wealthy. She had been to a museum once, seen cars that needed a driver, someone to steer it. They were carefully preserved in large glass cases, sterile and lifeless. She had taken Max, but he was too young really, was more interested in the animated games in the entrance foyer.

Perhaps the roads on the island were too rough for cars, or perhaps the wind farm did not produce enough electricity. She had not asked about that yet. The rest of the world used the grid, the electricity from the solar farms in the East. Great panels that stretched across deserts, sending power around the globe. She had seen pictures, they seemed vast, never ending.

The need for sustainable power was one of the reasons the Global Council had been formed. People had begun to realise that if their species was to remain, to not become extinct, there needed to be greater cooperation. Historical events, like summits of world leaders, took on greater significance, everyone watched, awaiting their decisions. Today, each country was part of a whole. The world worked together, the Global Council decided policies for everyone. They had halted climate change before it was too late, had tackled many of the social problems around the world. War and famine were things from long ago, barely remembered even by the very oldest people.

The sky was high and blue with small clouds scudding quickly across it, almost like another sea with foamy waves chasing each other but higher, slower. Seagulls circled in their noisy quest for food.

They found a spot, sheltered by the dunes, not too windy, and Lena sat, hugging her jacket closer. Lucy had brought an empty pot, the closest they could come to a bucket, and began to collect small shells and stones. Max wandered to the water's edge and began to throw stones at the waves. Lena watched his angry back as his arm arched over, the missiles shooting straight and long. She sighed. He was so like his father, felt everything deeply, refused to compromise. She hoped he would stay dry.

They had more clothes now, a change of everything that she could wash and dry ready for the next day, but she was not keen to do laundry unnecessarily. She had asked Agnes how they should pay, if no one used bar codes on the island. She had been told that they were not banned, that sometimes they *did* use them to pay for things from the mainland. But not this time. The fisherman had given the things freely, they weren't new, had been collected from the back of someone's cupboard. This was not a comfortable thought, and not one that she shared with the children. Lena was not used to being helped.

Lucy had wandered down to the wet sand and was scooping great heaps of it into her pot, turning it up to make a sandcastle. Lena remembered doing that herself, making great cities of sand with her father. They always built them on an inlet, where water was running to the sea, somewhere the sandy landscape would be constantly changing. Sometimes they would try to divert the river, pitching their speed and skill against the flow of the water. They never won but it was fun to try, to use up urgent energy in a quest, working together, getting warm and damp, while her mother sat shivering nearby, asking when they could leave.

Max had begun to wander along the sea edge and she was about to call to him, to tell him not to go too far or too near the water, when she saw her.

The woman was walking on the dry sand, heading towards them but with her head bent so she could not see them. She wore jeans, a jacket and a hijab. The scarf covered her head and was flapping in the wind, as though it would be torn away and dance across the sand. She saw Max and stopped. A frozen image. She scanned the beach, noticing Lucy and Lena. She changed direction and began to approach.

Lena was unsure about this. She could hardly remember seeing anyone with such a public display of a faith. So much of the way that society operated now was based on the abolition of strong belief.

That had started years ago, before Lena was even born. If you looked at history, there had always been wars and unrest due to religion, from the time of the crusades, possibly even earlier. There had been the trouble in Ireland over Catholics and Protestants, later there had been Islamic extremists causing terrors throughout the world. Eventually that world had decided it had had enough. It decreed that whilst faith was allowable, to be encouraged even, extreme views of any kind were dangerous. A new religion had grown up, a sort of amalgamation of all the faiths mixed up together, the idea that everyone could meet together and pray, and who or what you prayed to was not important. It became acceptable to be religious, to believe what you wanted, but that belief must not be exclusive. To say there was *one* God, to say other's beliefs were wrong, became almost equivalent to treason.

People adjusted. Churches, temples, synagogues, mosques all either closed or followed the new rules. People met in Holy Places, converted spaces that had all the major icons from the main faiths. Most people seemed happy, harmonious. The few who disagreed were very quiet or disappeared or were altered. There were a lot of altered people in the first few years, some returned to their homes and some did not. No one openly discussed religion, it was too dangerous, you never knew who might be listening. People could still meet together, still pray. John and Agnes prayed before every meal, completely openly. But there were no strong views discussed. Ever. Lena knew her husband had held dangerous views, knew that he refused to cooperate with the new laws. She was hazy on some of his beliefs, but she knew that they were uncompromising, and assumed that this was why she was here, assumed that this was an island that helped those who believed in only one God, who would not or could not forsake that faith.

So, why was a Muslim here? Had she misunderstood everything about the island? Nothing had been said, it was all an assumption, maybe a wrong one.

Suddenly, she did not want to speak to this woman, this wearer of a garment that shouted to the world that she would not compromise on faith, who seemed militant simply by her very apparel. Separate, refusing to be part of society. Lena privately blamed the Muslims for the current laws, felt that it was the number of terrorist attacks done in the name of Islam that had finally pushed the Global Council towards criminalising belief. Muslims were therefore to blame for her husband's removal. If the laws were less strict, her husband would be with her, at home where they belonged.

She stood, hitching her jeans, maybe she had lost weight, maybe they were the wrong size. Facing her children and cupping her hands around her mouth so the wind would not scatter her words, she called for Max and Lucy to come. They came, unexpectedly obedient, perhaps recognising that her tone was urgent, rarely used. She told them they needed to leave, offered no explanation and began to stride back towards the cottage. The children followed, muttering about spoiled games, not enough time, couldn't she make up her mind.

Leaving the children to shake the sand from their socks in the garden, she marched into the kitchen. Agnes was there. Agnes was always there, trapped by the need to provide food for five people. She saw Lena's face and stopped kneading bread. For a moment. Then she lowered her gaze to the table, pushed the dough into a new shape and asked her what had happened.

Lena sank into a chair.

"I don't understand why I'm here," she said, "and I don't know what this place is. I saw a Muslim wearing a hijab on the beach." She stopped. She could not put her tangled thoughts into words, couldn't find a way to express that she was battered inside, everything was too new, too strange and she did not know what to believe. She had thought she understood the island, had thought it was because of her husband's faith that she was here. So why was a Muslim sharing the same space? And if she was wrong about that, what else was she wrong about?

Agnes pulled off a piece of dough, rolled it in flour, shaped it into a ball. She spread oil across a baking sheet, placed the roll at the edge. Gave her time to pause, to think, to calm down. When she spoke it was with the same quiet tone that she always used, as though she had all the time in the world, all the patience in the world, had seen all there was to see in the world. Maybe she had.

"Ah, that would be Nargis, she often walks on the beach. You would like her I think, she is about your age. She lost her children though and we weren't able to get them back. Poor girl, broke her heart. She isn't ready to leave yet."

Her words sliced straight to Lena's heart like a physical wound. She had lost her children. In that one sentence she lost the label 'Muslim' and took on the new one of 'mother'. A label that Lena understood, felt, was part of. Agnes was speaking again, gently chiding her, guessing her thoughts.

"Lena, you have many things to get used to and lots to learn. You have been fed lies for a very long time, it must be hard to trust again. But really, we are here to try and help you, to get you and the children somewhere safe. As soon as we know about your husband, whether he can join you, we will arrange for you to move on. Do try not to worry dear.

"And Nargis? Well, try to remember, there are many many grains of sand, many many stars."

Chapter Two

The Plan

Lena woke to the sound of the wind farm. Both children still slept, so she stayed where she was. Max was beginning to make a fuss about sleeping in the same room. He wanted her to ask Agnes if he could sleep on the sofa. But Lena felt they were imposition enough, did not want to cause more disturbance than they already had, told him he would survive, it wasn't for long. She reached out her hand for the little book on the bedside table. The table was littered now with their possessions, toothbrushes, bottles of shampoo, brushes, combs, all fighting for space on the tiny square surface.

The system of obtaining items seemed tortuous compared with the ease of simply ordering them when at home. Agnes had explained that as they had not been classified as criminals, in theory they were still completely at liberty to go back to the mainland to shop. However, they would now be viewed by most officials as 'ill', needing medical attention. That could well lead to treatment which would involve altering. She was very frightened by the thought of alteration, fearing she would stop being herself.

Lena felt that you tended to define yourself by how your brain worked, your thoughts, how you responded to things, emotions. It was all stored in the brain. If they altered it, did you stop being yourself? Were you in effect obliterated, leaving only a body as a shell? She had asked John about it. He said they had successfully managed to change criminal behaviour in over 75% of cases, but they had never managed to change belief. Even when the alteration went wrong, when they left someone a dependent, or with no memory, or no ability to make decisions, they still retained the same basic belief system. As he pointed out, even a young child can believe in God. It is not necessarily a mental thing. He said that it would not be long before they stopped doing alterations for belief.

Lena opened the little book, a Bible. It was so long since she had held one. They were available online of course, everything was available online. But they often had sections edited out, it was not easy to know if you were reading an authentic version. There was something special about holding a book, turning the thin pages, letting the words wash over her. The book was very old. All books had ceased to be printed years ago, considered an unnecessary waste of resources. They were available for viewing in museums, but you couldn't touch them, turn the pages. A few people owned them; they were highly valuable, sold at auction for thousands, collector's pieces, far removed from their original purpose.

It was a while since she had read the Bible, thought about God in a real way in fact. Ironic, when that was probably the reason she had lost her husband, had needed to leave her home. Sometimes it was hard to think beyond the immediate, to turn your mind to somewhere higher, to keep life in perspective. So easy to get stuck in the present, the physical, to worry only about how long the toothpaste would last and whether the children would need new shoes before they could order them. To worry about where her husband was and how she would cope if forced to raise the children alone. No, she needed some time to think, to pray, to get her mind back to the right place. She smiled grimly. If she couldn't, they wouldn't need to bother altering her, she would be a mental wreck anyway.

She swung her legs out of bed, reached for her clothes, tip-toed to the bathroom. She would walk along the coast, clear her head, talk to God. Try to get herself straightened out.

#

Max heard her go but lay very still, kept his breathing even, his eyes shut. He listened to the door close, the sounds in the

31

bathroom, her footsteps downstairs. When he was sure that he was safe, he carefully stood, the blanket falling to the ground, picked up his clothes and traced her steps to the bathroom. He was fed up with having to share a room, disliking the close proximity enforced on them every day since they had arrived. He was also worried about his father. No one had told Max anything, they treated him like a child, not someone who was almost as tall as his mother, someone whose voice was already becoming lower, more manly. He knew that both his parents had gone to the hospital and that only one had returned. Had been told that his father was well but may not be free to leave the hospital, that he should not discuss it with his friends, they would just have to wait and see. He had no idea what was wrong, if his father had some strange disease, had committed some crime or maybe had simply left them. But he intended to find out.

He thought he could find his way back to the cave that led to the tunnel. There had been no guards, no security. The most difficult part would be leaving the guesthouse at the other end. He would just have to hope to be lucky there, to slink through the house and hope he wasn't seen. His computer – small, blue, comforting, a link to the real world – was in his room, he could pick it up and hope to leave.

The walk through the tunnel had been long and difficult but he would be better prepared this time, he wouldn't rush into anything, would take a few days to plan it. If he started to collect food now, some warm clothes, a torch, then things would be easier. He had not noticed any turnings in the tunnel, thought it was a single route back to the guesthouse. He would not need to rush, could stop for breaks to rest. And of course he could go during the day, not in the middle of the night when his body just wanted to sleep. He needed to think of an excuse, a reason to be missing for a whole day. Then his mother wouldn't start to look for him until evening. Perhaps he could befriend a fisherman, he could tell his mother that he was going to have a trip on the boat for a day. That would give him some time.

He was unsure about what would happen when he arrived back in town. If he could get home, he knew the code for the door lock and that it worked on his thumb print as well as his parents. He could rest a bit, then text for a car and go to the hospital. The cost would simply be added to his parents' account if he showed a bar code, and he had seen his mother put hers into the back of the little book she was reading. That would get him to the hospital. What would happen after that was still unclear. Never mind, he could think about it some more, plan it a bit better. First he needed to check the cave was where he thought it was. Then he needed to start making friends with one of the fishermen. They stopped in the little harbour most days; he would walk there now, before Lucy woke up and insisted on coming. She would get in the way.

He dressed quickly, carrying his shoes as far as the kitchen door so as to be as quiet as possible. He pushed his feet into them, opened the door and was outside. He had no way of knowing which way his mother would walk so he set off towards the cave, hoping to avoid her. The harbour was in the other direction so he would have to risk passing the cottage again but he thought that was okay. If anyone saw him he could say he was walking, looking for shells or something. He did not think anyone would be stupid enough to believe he would be remotely interested in shells but you never knew, grownups could be pretty dim sometimes.

He tried whistling as he walked. A boy at school could do it, could whistle whole tunes. Max thought that was pretty cool. He couldn't manage much more than a hiss – it sounded like he was imitating the wind. He screwed up his face, puckering his lips as he tried to find the correct shape for his mouth. The sound refused to change, it was irritating and he stopped, he had other things to think about.

One of his socks had crept down into his shoe, making his foot rub against the heel. He stopped to pull it up, overbalancing and stepping onto the wet sand. Bother. Now his foot was damp and sandy as well as sore at the back. He hadn't even found the cave yet. This was beginning to be less exciting, less of an adventure, more of an uncomfortable exercise in stamina. He wished he'd thought to bring some food from the kitchen, a man couldn't be expected to do much before breakfast. Agnes – Old Aggie he called her in his head, where his mother couldn't hear – was not a bad cook. He liked the food, fresh, hot, different. It didn't taste like the food at home, which always had that slightly plasticky tang of reheated food. Wished his mother would cook. Wished his mother would do a lot of things. Like talk to him, treat him like an adult instead of lumping him and little Lucy together. Lucy Loo-Seat he called her, just to make her squeal. No, he wasn't a child. He would be as tall as his mother within a year, surely that should come with some rights.

He had left the dunes far behind now and was walking along the edge of the cliffs. They were a mix of sand and rock, fallen down in places, great swathes of field tumbled onto the beach. Gradually the sandstone changed to harder rock, he knew he must be getting near. There were folds and shadows in the rock face, the sun was facing him, dazzling in his eyes, making it hard to see far ahead, reflecting off the sea, making the rock look very black. He was almost level with the cave when he saw it, gaping towards the sea. It was smaller than he remembered, he had to stoop slightly to go inside, then three stone steps down, covered in debris from the sea – old seaweed, empty shells, pebbles and sand, all washed in a muddle over the first few steps. Then the floor sloping upwards, away from the sea, beyond the reach of even the highest tide and then, gradually, hardly discernible, sloping down and down and away. It was not exactly as he remembered but then it had been late, he had been tired. It was the right cave though; he was sure of that. He wondered how long he had been there. No mobile, so no way of checking. Stupid island, was like living in the last century. He would bring his pocket computer back with him when he came. He could fill a backpack with a few essentials, make the time go a bit faster. His own underwear too, I mean, who wants to wear pants someone other than your mum has bought? It wasn't right.

He turned, started walking back towards the cottage. No need to mark the way, he'd be coming in daylight, would be easy enough to find again. As he walked he began to list the things he would need to bring. Some food, a torch, a coat, the bar code, some water, a bag to put it all in. He could ask Old Aggie for one. That should do it. It wouldn't be hard to find those things. He would leave the bar code until the morning he left, give his mother less time to notice it was missing.

He felt quite cheerful now. It was a good plan. He could find out where his father was, tell him about the island, bring him back. If he was too ill to travel well, at least he would know, could stop blaming his mother. He could let his mates know too, they would be wondering where he had gone, why he hadn't buzzed them recently, wouldn't guess he had no computer. After all, who doesn't have a computer? Was unheard of.

As he approached the cottage he could smell bacon frying. Probably best to eat breakfast before he went to the harbour, he wasn't too sure how easy it would be to befriend a fisherman, he might have to watch them work for a while, pretend to be interested in boats or something. He stood, smelling the bacon, deciding how he felt. His heel had a blister, could sort that out, let his mother see he was safe, eat, then go a bit later. Maybe have bit of a rest too. There was a lot to organise, didn't want to rush it.

He crossed the lawn, opened the kitchen door. Agnes looked round in surprise. He removed his wet shoes, said he had wanted some exercise, gave her his most angelic smile and sat at the table, waiting for his food.

The Mission

Three days later, Max was ready. He had collected food and placed it in a bag that Agnes had given to him for collecting shells. He had not walked as far as the harbour but he had told his mother that he had, said he had befriended a fisherman and asked permission to go out on his boat. She had refused, of course, but when he went missing that is the first place she would look for him, earning him extra time.

He would have liked to use John's computer, to search the hospital records, find out exactly where his father was, but John tended to keep it in his study when he was not using it. Max had tried to use it while John was out digging the garden, which seemed an almost constant activity. But the study door was locked and the key code would not recognise his thumbprint. To Max's mind, that in itself was suspect. Why would anyone have a door in their own house which needed to be kept locked? What secrets did he keep in there? It confirmed more than ever the necessity of his plan, the need to get his father here. His dad would not be fooled by anyone, he was not as trusting as his mum, who clearly needed to be rescued from the situation she had brought them all into.

His mother was still sleeping. He could hear her breath, even and calm, in and out, in and out. He needed to wait until she had woken. She had taken to a habit of reading the little book then going for a walk before breakfast. He had not dared to remove the bar code the night before, in case she noticed it was missing. Now he needed her to wake, read and leave. Then he could begin to put his plan into action. She seemed to be sleeping extremely late. He lay on his makeshift bed on the floor, feeling its hardness reaching through the thin blanket, pressing against his shoulder blades. A sofa would be much more comfortable, much more private. His dad would probably be prepared to ask if Max could sleep separately. He would understand that it was not right for a boy to share rooms with his mother and sister.

At last, she woke. Max lay very still, listening to the first stirrings as she stretched, yawned, eased from the bed, crept to the bathroom. Sounds of water running, of flushing, of teeth being scrubbed. Then the scrape of the door as it was gently pushed open, her light footsteps as she returned to the bed, the flutter of pages being turned. He felt he could almost hear her concentration as she read. He lay flat, concentrating on breathing evenly, trying to keep still, ignoring an itch on his foot, a stiff muscle in one arm. Then, finally, finally, she gathered her clothes and left the room. He counted slowly to twenty, forcing himself to not move until her footsteps had left the stairs, moved further away.

Moving slowly, *must not wake Lucy*, inching towards the table, not even breathing. Picking up the book, opening the cover, sliding out the narrow strip of the bar code. It was hard in his hand, the plastic coating digging into his palm as he gathered his clothes, checked his torch was still in his pocket, crept from the room.

The bag was where he had left it, hidden behind a rock in the garden. It was wet with dew but the contents seemed untouched. Not much, a snack really, a bottle of water, something to keep up his strength. He did not need it yet, was too tense to eat, a tight knot in his stomach, a slight ache in his head. He was nervous about going back into that tunnel, that confined damp space of darkness. Afraid of what might lurk in the dark corners, watching him.

He told himself he was being silly, being a baby, letting his imagination get the better of him. He was the man of the family now, wasn't that what everyone kept telling him? Now he needed to rescue the other man, get the family back on track. He walked along the path to the beach. It was dry but windy, always windy. The sand whipped up, swirling around his feet, occasionally dancing higher, stinging his eyes, gritty on his lips. He hated this place.

He crossed the dunes, smelling the heavy tang of sea and salt and dead fish. His feet sinking into the dried sand, filling his socks, scratching his feet, crowding his toes. Never mind, he could empty his shoes when he got to the cave. The long grass danced in the wind, a frantic, whirling dance, mocking his journey, knowing he would fail.

He ignored the grass with its sharp edges and vicious dance, trudged on to the beach. The bag was annoying in his hand, the plastic damp against his skin. He could feel the hard water bottle inside, knocking against his leg as he walked, bump bump bump. Changing the rhythm of his steps, trying to slow him, to make him stop. He felt that everything was against him, the sighing grass whispering that he should return, the bottle bouncing, laughing at his attempts, the sea rushing towards him in great leaps then withdrawing in alarm, warning him to turn around.

He would not listen, he would not look. It was not real. It was because he was tired, had hardly slept last night, had eaten very little while his plan fizzed and bubbled in his stomach. He would be alright when he got to the cave. The darkness would hide him, calm him, help him to keep going.

He trudged across the beach, his feet sliding occasionally on the large rocks, the sand in his socks rubbing, uncomfortable, making his steps awkward. Some had worked into the cut on his heel and it was stinging. He wanted to turn around, to trust himself to the care of his mother, to shut off his worries as his sister seemed to have done. But something made him go forward, reminded him that he was a man now. A man who wanted his father. And his computer.

It was not right to live such an isolated life. He knew that community was what mattered, unity was everything. He heard it regularly at school sessions, on the computer screenings, on the flash adverts. His whole life he had been told that the global community, man helping man, working as a single unit, that was what mattered. That was what had enabled mankind to survive, to not become extinct like so many of the animals they learned about in school. He had seen films of great striped cats that in the past had lived in the wild and now lived only as a few cells in a test tube, pieces of DNA that they hoped to one day be able to develop into an animal again, to clone new versions of an old species. This was the fate that man had learned to avoid for himself. Max agreed it was necessary, he was a responsible unit in the global community.

He was at the cave now, feeling the salty coldness as he went inside, smelling seaweed and stale air. He sat and emptied his socks, making a small heap of sand on the hard rock floor. Rubbing his toes with his fingers, making the skin gritty, wiping it on his trousers. He could not remove all of it, his socks still felt rough when he put them back on. His mother always managed to remove the sand from their feet, rubbing them roughly with her hand until every last grain had fallen. But his mother was not here now. He was on a mission to rescue her. A little sand between the toes was not such a big deal, he could ignore it, press onwards.

He stood again, too quickly, grazed his head on the low rock roof. It hurt, made him feel weaker. No one knew, no one saw him be hurt. He wished even his sister was with him, even in her silliness she would be company, would be concerned that he had struck his head. He wondered if he could go back for her, persuade her to come with him. But she was too young, she would complain on the walk, tell him she was tired, ask him for piggyback rides, probably tell his mother his plan. Or even tell Aggie, his sister seemed to have formed an attachment to the old woman, was often found sitting at the kitchen table, learning how to cook, watching her work, chatting in her careless girl manner, scattering facts about their lives. No, better to go alone.

He reached into his pocket and pulled out the torch, turned it on. He had found it in an old shed next to the house. It was old fashioned, recharged from the mains, heavy in his hand. The beam shone weakly in the gloom, casting a yellow light across the rocks. He walked forwards into the cave, first up the slope away from the sea, away from the sand. Soon he could hardly hear the waves and he found the steps, leading downwards. They were great slabs of rock, higher than was comfortable. It had been easier going up them than down. He turned slightly sideways, he did not want to fall, no one would find him.

He dropped down each giant step, holding onto the slippery rock wall to keep his balance. Then reached the level floor below. It dipped away, taking him further down. He was aware this time of how deep he was going, felt the weight of the earth above him like a physical pressure. He imagined the ceiling caving in, the earth rushing to bury him, to push the life out of him, steal his air and his strength.

Again, he nearly turned, nearly fled back to the safety of his hard bed, the comfort of the breakfast that would soon be served. No one would know, they would think he had come back from a walk, the same as the last two mornings. They would not wonder, not be alarmed. But he would have failed. He would be stuck on that island, knowing nothing, with no means of communication. No, he could do this, he could go on. Nothing was collapsing except for his courage. He was not a baby.

On he walked. Twice he slipped on the smooth rock, bruised his knees, jarred his wrists. But he did not cry out, knowing that no one could hear him. He kept hold of the torch. He was ever aware of the sea above him, imagined it hurling towards him, forced himself to not think, not wonder. The torch seemed very weak, its beam yellow and faint against the rock walls. He wondered what he would do if it died, wished he had thought to recharge it fully. He turned it off at one point, wanted to see if it was still possible to go forward, if there was any light at all. The darkness rushed at him, pressed against his eyes. He felt breath against his face, knew a monster was there, flicked the torch back on. There was nothing but rock, shining in the yellow beam that trembled now as his hand shook. On, on, he forced himself on.

Then the floor began to change and he knew he was rising, was not as deep as before. He must be nearing the guesthouse, his walk nearly complete. He stopped. The wall on one side had gone. He shone the torch. There was another passage, leading off to his right. This was unexpected. He had seen only one route when they came, had not noticed any choices, any tunnels other than the one they had walked. Which route was correct? He shone the torch on the floor but there were no clues, both routes had smooth rock, he assumed they had been carved centuries before. He tried to think.

When they had come they had walked in pairs, the adults afraid the children might slip. He had walked with his mother, her slightly in front, following the girl and his sister. He had held his mother's right hand, so he must have walked on what was now the left side of the tunnel. He would not therefore have seen the other route. Was that right? If they had walked the other way, would he have seen the tunnel he was in? No, he was tired, but he was confident he was correct. If his left hand had held his mother's right, the wall would have continued at his side as one continuous wall. He would not have seen the other opening, he could continue on the route he was on. He wondered where the other tunnel went, if it was a better path. He did not feel inclined to find out.

As he neared the guesthouse he began to plan. He would exit the bathroom, collect their things from the room and then text for a car to take him home.

He stopped, his feet still, his heart pounding.

When they had entered the tunnel, been rushed at night from their sleep, led away, the girl had unlocked the cupboard door. It had been locked. From the outside. If, when she returned after delivering them, she had locked it on her departure – and why wouldn't she – then he was trapped. There was no way out from the staircase. He could hardly hammer on the door.

He felt sick, worried that he might actually throw up. He sat. The rock was hard and cold but he barely noticed. How could he have been so silly? So childish. Why had this only occurred to him now, when he had walked so far? Should he retrace his steps, follow the other tunnel? But he had no idea where it went, or even if it was safe. He did not want to die down here, lost forever in a maze of darkness.

The torch flickered. That decided him. Soon the battery would be completely empty. He would go on, forwards, be sure of the situation before he made a plan. If the door was locked, perhaps he could force it open, it was at least worth a try. He was not convinced that he could find a solution so he decided to ignore the problem, to simply not think about it.

He had come to the steps up now. They were big, great strides up, one step at a time. Then he recognised that he was inside the house, moving between the walls. The air was warmer, fresher; he fancied he could hear sounds. It felt better to be near life again, even if separated from it by thick walls. He came to the attic, crossed the wooden floor, enjoying the feel of something new beneath his feet. The tension inside him was growing, he had no plans. If the door was locked he was stuck. The torch was off but he was not sure how much battery was left, not sure if he was brave enough to attempt the black tunnels without a light.

Then the steps down. He was careful to move quietly, to not rush. He could see the door now and slowed even more, not sure if he wanted to know if it was locked, if he was trapped. He arrived. His hand shook as he reached up, took the latch in his damp hand, held his breath and pressed it.

The Journey Continues

Max pushed his thumb on the latch and it clicked open. He leaned on the door. Nothing happened. Feeling panic begin to rise in his stomach, he leaned with more force. The door swung open, he lost his balance, fell out of the staircase, banged his knee on the toilet lid and landed in a heap on the floor. The sense of relief that surged through him almost made him cry. Almost. He sat for a moment just breathing, enjoying the sunlight that flooded through the little window, the warmth of the floor beneath him. He had done it, the first part of his plan was finished.

He stood up, resting against the closed toilet for a minute, still felt a little shaky. Then, worried someone might come, he locked the door, good thought. He could have a drink, use the toilet, then set about collecting their stuff from the room. That was stage two. It helped now to think of the plan in stages, pretend he was ticking off the parts he had accomplished. It stopped him thinking too far ahead, worrying about the bits which were still a bit fuzzy, a bit vaguer than he felt comfortable with. He had always found not thinking too much to be the best method. It was where women went wrong, they thought about everything, made them worry, when most of the time there was nothing to be concerned about.

Ignoring the stabbing doubt that maybe in this case there *was* something to worry about, he went to the little sink. The water was cold and sweet when he put his mouth under the tap. Best drink he had ever tasted. If he had glanced in the mirror above the sink, he would have seen that he had a dark smudge of dirt on one cheek, his hair was damp and unkempt and his eyes looked especially large in his pale face. But he did not look, he was a boy, they don't do things like that.

He unlocked the door and peered round it. The corridor smelt of carpet shampoo and dried flowers. No one was in sight, good. He edged out of the door and made for the stairs, as quietly as he could without looking suspicious, he wanted anyone who saw him to think he was a guest, allowed to be here. Which was correct, he was. He had to keep reminding himself of that, he was not trespassing, he was a paying guest. He actually had absolutely no idea how long his mother had booked the rooms for, but that was one of those things not worth thinking about.

He reached the second floor, found his room, pressed his thumb against the lock pad. Nothing. The tiny red light stayed lit, watching him, knowing his was the wrong thumb, not allowing him to enter. He tried his mother's door, they had all been programmed together, so they could all open each other's rooms. Still nothing. This was unexpected. He heard voices in the hallway below, jovial, discussing the weather. They might decide to come up so he went back upstairs, must not run, just a fast walk, into the little bathroom, lock the door. He sat back on the toilet and put his head in his hands, stared at his feet. Now what?

They must have noticed the family had gone, or maybe they were only booked in for one night. He wished he had asked. If they were using the room for other guests, they would have cleared out all their belongings. They would not have thrown them away. They would either have returned them to their home or kept them. He was going to hope they had kept them. He needed that computer, couldn't order a car without one. There must be an office,

44

somewhere secure, where valuables would be put. He decided to go and look.

The wide staircase ran down to the main hall, carpeted in the centre, edges of oak showing at the sides. From the bottom stair ran a long tiled hallway, at the end there was a double-fronted door. He could see through the part-glazed door to the driveway, which was edged with lawns. On either side of the hall were doors, one leading to the dining room, already set for dinner, with white cloths and peach napkins folded into fans. The other door led to a lounge, big sofas arranged around coffee tables, large flower arrangements, power sockets for recharging electronics. He knew both these rooms so could ignore them. There was another, narrow corridor which ran along the back of the house. At one end there was a room with large windows. It looked out onto the gardens and was full of simulation games as well as some antique activities, like darts and table tennis. Nothing of value would be put in there.

The other end of the narrow corridor led to steps, which ducked below the staircase he was on and curved downwards. They were used by the staff. Max went down. The stairs were narrow and twisted, he hoped he wouldn't meet anyone coming up. He came to a short landing with two rooms. The stairs continued down. He could smell food cooking and hear voices; there must be the kitchens down there. The smell of food, rich and salty, reminded him he was hungry. Afraid that there would also be people, he decided to go no lower. He looked into the room next to him, pushing the door open a crack and peering round. It was an office and it was empty.

Max leaped inside, saw there was an old fashioned lock with a key and turned it. He then realised that should someone come, that would look more suspicious, so he unlocked it but left the door closed. He turned to the room. There was a huge desk holding three computers, their detachable keypads sitting beside them. One was facing a blank wall, ready to project images. If he failed to find his own computer, he could use one to order a car.

He walked soundlessly across the faded green carpet, past the dark furniture. A round table sat solidly in the middle of the room, holding a display case with three open books. There was a large cupboard, locked, and a glass case holding a display of more books, their spines faded. Max wondered why anyone would invest in such things. On the walls were photographs of the guesthouse through the ages. He glanced at them as he passed, seeing the house change with the times, the transport on the drive ageing the building. It was old, really old.

Then he saw it. There, tucked away in the corner, was his mother's case. He lifted it. It was heavy, good, must be full of their stuff. He picked it up, carried it to the door, checked for people. The corridor was still empty so he heaved the case back up the dark winding stairs, along the corridor, up the wide staircase, back to the safety of the bathroom. It was heavy, it bumped against the stairs as he struggled with it but he made it. Boy and case arrived unseen.

There was just enough floor space to open the case and rummage through the clothes and computers. There was his computer, like an old friend, sitting in the bottom of the case, next to Lucy's socks. He pulled it out, gave it a wipe and turned it on. Then he found the number for the car company.

He thought for a moment. Usually they used the cheapest grade of cars. These were guaranteed to arrive within twenty minutes and would take you short distances. However, while they would get you to your intended destination within an hour, if someone else ordered the same grade car and was en route, they would detour and collect the second passenger too. They tended to be large, holding eight or ten people. He and Lucy both used them when they had school sessions. They were cheap and could be fun if travelling with your mates. But people tended to chat. A boy travelling that distance alone was bound to cause questions. He did not want questions.

The next grade of car offered the same timings and was also cleaned at the end of the day, not between customers. However, it would take you directly to your destination, you did not have to share the journey with other passengers. Max decided that this was the best option.

He would have liked to use the more expensive cars, the ones that were cleaned between each customer, that were built to resemble antique cars, were extra comfortable and rather beautiful. But his mother might kill him and he was probably in enough trouble already.

He sent the text order, waited fifteen minutes in the bathroom (so nice to have his computer again, to know times) then walked downstairs and out the front door. He left the case where it lay, no point in heaving around his mother's and sister's clothes. No one saw him; he could hardly believe how lucky he had been.

The car was waiting, he compared the number on top with the number he had in his reply text, it was his car. He sat inside and slid his mother's bar code under the small scanner. The red light flickered over it, then turned green, letting him know the fee was paid. Had the amount been less, he could have used his own bar code.

The spending limits were set by the parents in each family. They could set the amount that children could spend without needing verification from an adult, the type of goods that they were allowed to buy. Max and Lucy had very low limits on their bar codes and no sugar-taxed food was allowed to be bought. Games, treats and viewing experiences were all limited. It had always annoyed Max, seemed unfair when his friends had greater freedoms than himself. Now he felt his point was proven – if his bar code had had higher spending limits, there would've been no need to 'borrow' his mother's.

He then looked at the address code screen, checking that the code he had texted was recorded correctly. It was. He had heard stories of people failing to check and not noticing they were being taken the wrong way, sometimes miles from where they wanted to go. He had heard of a family going all the way to Italy, but he doubted that was true. How could you fail to notice if you went through one of the inter-country tunnels?

He checked the on-board camera was off, the one you could use if there was a problem, if the car stopped or you needed help. It had a big sign above it, warning of dire consequences if it was misused. It was off, so Max could continue unseen unless they chanced to do a spot check on his particular car.

As soon as he clicked his seat belt into place the car moved forwards, slowly along the driveway, then turned onto the main road and headed towards his home. Max sat back on his seat and breathed a long sigh. The floor was littered with someone's sweet wrappers and his seat was slightly sticky. But he didn't care. Stage two was complete.

#

When Max's car left the guesthouse, the man watching from the lounge window turned away. He frowned. This would need to be handled very carefully. He went down to the kitchen area and informed the staff they could continue with their day, there was no need to stay out of sight any longer. Then he went to his office. As expected, the fawn suitcase was no longer in the corner. He was surprised the boy had managed it so quietly.

He went to the desk and entered his security code to turn on the computer, paused, chose his words with care, then wrote the email. He had some sympathy for the boy, he was too young for this

48

really. However, they had very little choice now. He read the email through twice, then sure it was sufficient, he pressed send.

He rose from the desk and stood for a moment, gazing at the framed photographs, the encased books. This house had seen many changes. He was a tall man, slim with dark hair. But his most noticeable feature was his eyebrows. They were very black and slanted upwards, giving him the appearance of an owl. A great horned owl.

Home

Max woke with a start. His head was banging against the car's window and his neck ached from being at a strange angle, he must have dozed off. He looked out of the window. The car was just beginning to enter the town, the change in speed must have been what woke him. He shuffled, uncomfortable in the seatbelt but knowing that if he unclicked it, even for a second, the car would stop and an automatic voice would tell him to refasten it. That might cause them to do a spot check, to turn on the on-board camera. He didn't want that, wanting to remain unseen.

He looked out of the window. Houses sped past. You could tell where you were in a town by the age of the houses. On the edge were the modern ones, always three or four stories high, always with greenery at every level, guttering designed to catch every rain drop and send them off to the main waterways beneath the ground. Then you came to the older houses, those built before the most recent technology. They tended to be lower, with roofs at a different pitch. Then, as you neared the centre of town, the houses were very old, centuries-old some of them. They were much sought after, carefully restored with all the latest heat reduction technology incorporated, but looking as they had for hundreds of years.

Of course, there were modern houses near the centre too, in places where older buildings had been demolished. The places where *libraries* or *shops* had once stood. (People used to actually go and collect items that they needed. They were displayed on shelves in large rooms and people selected what they wanted, paid and then carried them home. Max had learned about it in history lessons. It must have taken them hours each week; he wondered how they managed to do anything else.) Some of these buildings had been turned into living spaces but most had been removed, replaced with something more useful. Space was always tight in a country as small as England and there was little room for indulgent preservation.

He was passing an old school now. The shell was preserved, but inside it had been converted into single unit homes for the elderly. He knew about schools, thought they would have been fun places to attend. They had lent their name to his own school sessions, though would have been very different, being taught by a teacher who was actually present.

In the past, there had been social experiments where children had been educated almost entirely remotely, all their lessons done on the computer, with links to a teacher who could see what they were doing and correct them if necessary or send different explanations. Everything was geared to the individual. The children studied at home or at their parent's work place.

However, it was then decided that this was unhealthy, that social interaction was a necessary part of development, good for the global community. Even the older children now attended some lessons each day for at least two hours. The rest of the day they were taught via computer link. The classes were staggered, so there was no need for the huge buildings of ancient times, when all the children in a whole town would be at school at the same time. Now they were in fixed classes, saw the same forty people every day for their school sessions. Each school session group, or class, was named after a country, part of the continual campaign to reduce the world, make the global community a unified mass. When they left, another session would use the same space. Max belonged to the Persia session, Lucy was in Russia. Once a year they would dress in their "country" ethnic costume, learn about their customs. In some ways it was effective, when Max had chanced to meet someone who did actually originate from Persia, he did feel a certain bond, a feeling of unity. It was all about unity.

They met in meeting centres, areas around town that could accommodate forty children and their computers. They had complicated driveways that allowed the cars to arrive and deliver, or await pick up, at the various change over times throughout the day. Some centres were complete science laboratories with all the latest equipment, some merely rooms with power points. There were art centres, music centres, technology centres, even language centres for those people who wanted to learn the indigenous languages of other countries. But everyone spoke English, so really that should, in Max's opinion, have been part of the history centre. The history centre was above a museum and they walked through displays of artefacts on their way to lessons. History was one of Max's favourite centres.

When not attending school sessions, he was free to work wherever his parents deemed was appropriate. All work places provided study rooms for the children of employees, and after the age of twelve they could choose to work at home if they wished.

The youngest children had longer sessions, in special play centres, full of toys where they could use their imaginations and also learn the first stages of computer use. They were driven in special 'child cars', which were always closely monitored, with seat belts that could not be unfastened when in motion and doors that remained locked until the appropriate adult used their bar code to release them.

Any pupil found on the street during study hours would have their bar code checked against the main computer terminal. If they did not have a legitimate reason for being on the street rather than studying, they would be punished. This usually involved the removal of all entertainment, both games and viewing experiences, for a set period. Of course, they could access this through a friend's or sibling's bar code, but if they were caught (and they often were, you never knew who was watching) then they too would be punished. For even longer. Very few people were willing to risk sharing bar codes.

At all school sessions there was always at least one teacher physically present, the others worked in elaborate studios, sending their lessons to thousands of children at the same time. They stood behind the great glass screens, explaining their lessons while images flickered across the glass, illustrating their points. Other teachers worked in checking centres, following what the pupils were doing online and giving extra input if it was necessary; or it was given by a bot, an intelligent machine that sounded like a person. Max and his friends often tried to confuse the bot. The bots were able to help with most routine problems, but if a student thought of something complex, something unexpected, they would have to be passed to an actual teacher for their questions to be answered.

Max suddenly gasped. He had completely forgotten about his school sessions. If he failed to log on or attend sessions, which he had, then he was expected to submit medical evidence of why. Would his mother have arranged this before their absence? He thought not. This meant that the authorities would start to look for him. If he decided to use his own bar code, it was quite likely they would trace him and someone would come to check what the problem was. He felt very angry with his mother, felt she had led them into an impossible situation. Never mind – he was on the way to rescuing them.

The car was nearing his house now. It seemed so long since they had left, though was actually hardly a week. The car stopped and he jumped out, checked he still had the bar codes, then shut the door. The car would wait the obligatory three minutes, in case he had left something and rushed back, but he ignored it and went to his front door.

The house was fairly modern, a slim frontage with three storeys in light brick. All the terraces in the road were the same. There were three fat steps up to the front door. Next to the door was the large white lock-box for hot food deliveries and a black one for parcels. There was also a basket, next to the third floor window, where delivery drones could drop parcels. In theory, this was a less secure delivery area as it was not locked. In practice, no one had ever been known to lose anything from the drone baskets. If deliveries weren't received it tended to be because they had been sent to the wrong address or the drone had malfunctioned somewhere along the way.

He held his mother's bar code under the sensor, pressed his thumb against the lock pad and the door swung open. He stepped inside. A rush of familiar smells greeted him, the carpet softly welcoming beneath his feet, the climate control at an ambient temperature, the lights coming on as he moved through the house, dimly because it was still light outside but comfortingly. He was home.

He walked through every room. There was no reason to do so, he just needed to see that everything was as they had left it, that their uncomfortable time on the island had not changed anything that mattered. Study: a room dominated by a large desk and computers. Lounge: sofas and plants arranged around low tables.

Dining area: the table and upright chairs deemed suitable for healthy eating. Kitchen: a line of cupboards for food, a microwave and hob, plus fridge and freezer. His mother did not cook, so no fancy cookers or work surfaces like some of his friends had in their homes. He reached into the first cupboard and pulled out some biscuits, ate them as he walked, crumbs scattering onto the carpet. Then upstairs, into his sister's room, toys (mostly pink) draped on every surface, mirrors covering the walls. His parents' room: tidy, white, mirrors and make up and the wonderful smell of their soap and perfumes.

Finally, into his own room. He stretched out on the bed, reaching for the switch to close his curtains, put on some music. He closed his eyes. He would rest, just for a minute. Then he would decide what to do at the hospital, how he was going to find his father.

He was tired after his long day, the walk, the tension, the relief of being home again. He would watch some entertainment, perhaps play a game, order some dinner. His father was not expecting him, there were no time constraints, he could afford to relax a little. He started to drift downwards into sleep, a whirl of images, a sense of floating, his breath shallow and even. Within minutes he was asleep.

#

The man outside the house watched the curtains close. He spoke into his phone, listened to instructions, settled down for a long wait.

Chapter Three

The Hospital

Max woke with a start. He lay for a moment, wondering what had woken him. He glanced at his clock, eight in the evening. He frowned, remembering where he was, why he had returned, feeling hungry. It was later than he had hoped but he could not do anything without food, eating was his first priority. He picked up his phone, ordered food. Hot food, but he was on a mission, was saving the family, his mother would not mind the expense. He used her bar code to pay. He flicked on the entertainment, choosing what to watch.

There were several different watching experiences that he could choose from. His parents had not paid for the more expensive options and he knew his friends all had more viewing experiences to choose from. Some of them also had illegal viewing experiences, especially those with older siblings.

The Global Council had some years ago banned anything that was deemed 'unhealthy', be that unhealthy for the individual's mind or unhealthy for the population as a whole. A link had been found between the watching of experiences that contained violence or sexual material and the behaviour of the watcher. They therefore removed both from the allowable viewing menu. They claimed it had reduced the number of unhealthy sexual liaisons and the amount of violent crime. Max had learned about it in Community Sessions. They had all listened carefully and completed the expected responses correctly in their online worksheets.

However, after the school session, while they were waiting for their cars, some of them had revealed that they had access to some of the forbidden material, that it did not turn them into crazed killers or sex perverts and if anyone wanted to borrow it they could. For a small fee.

Max had watched one at a friend's house, the group of boys huddled excitedly in comfy chairs while the images were projected onto a wall. It contained fight scenes involving weapons and several characters died. It had been made many years ago and the quality was inferior to those he was used to watching. There was no 3-D option and the sound quality was passable but unrealistic in places. However, he was glad he had seen one and Max did not feel he had been turned into a killer. It was exciting, interesting, had stayed in his mind for several days afterwards. However, he was not sure he liked it, had not joined his friends for subsequent viewings. He did not like the thought that life could be so easily ended.

Now, he flicked aimlessly through the different experiences. None of them captivated him. Time meandered forwards. There was a buzz at the door, his food had arrived.

He went to the door, one sock had come off and remained on his bed. He walked feeling lopsided, the bare foot noticing the wooden floor, the rough carpet, the cold tiles. The man at the door handed him his food. He was not wearing the food delivery shirt, which struck Max as unusual but he seemed friendly enough, smiled, hoped Max would enjoy his dinner, waved and left. Max carried the large insulated white box through to the dining area. He did not bother with plates, just pulled cutlery from a drawer and poured a glass of juice from the tap. The pasta and meat were packed separately in small cardboard containers, lined with silvery foil. He peeled the lid from each and ate. He was hungry. He sat at the table, one foot curled beneath him, the one without a sock. He did not think about eating in a different room, his mother would not have liked it.

It was even later than he had planned by the time he had eaten. He pushed the dirty boxes to the centre of the table and buried his head in his hands. He needed to think. He had no idea how to find which area of the hospital his father would be in. Nor did he feel he should ask at the registration desk, knowing instinctively that there was something not good about his parent's hospital visit, that somehow it had been the cause for his mother's hasty decision to take them to the guesthouse and then the island. He ran his hands through his hair, rubbed his eyes. It was too difficult. He could not plan, he would make it up as he went. He ordered a car and went into the bathroom. His reflection stared back at him, tense and ruffled with a dirty smudge on his cheek and a piece of meat sauce just below his lip. He decided he might need to look young and cute, it was often useful when trying to convince adults about things. He combed his hair, washed his face, practised doing big-eyed poses to himself, grinned showing his one crooked tooth, pursed his lips and looked as if he might cry at any moment. He decided it was convincing enough. He found a jacket, his missing sock and pulled on his shoes. He was waiting by the door when the car arrived.

The sky was dark, reflecting the yellow lights. He could still see clearly, every street well lit. The streetlights would remain lit until dawn, causing dark shadows in passing gardens and side passages but illuminating the walkways and roads to almost daytime brightness. The hospital was even brighter, shining like a beacon to guide them from some distance. It was set on a slight hill and could easily be seen several minutes before he arrived. The car followed the road as it wound upwards, turning past the various dismounting bays. Max had put in the address for the visitor's entrance and he was dropped at the door. He climbed out, checked he still had both bar codes and walked into the hospital.

As he entered the building, a fine spray of germ killing mist engulfed him. When he left (it did not occur to him that he might not leave) through the exit door, a similar spray of 'good bacteria' would counteract the effects. Virulent germs were a problem these days. Max had learnt in science sessions how there had been a time when people used bacteria-killing gels and soaps without constraint, how every household had used liquid soaps, trying to eradicate germs. The problem was that they only killed *most* of the germs, never a full 100%. The remaining bacteria had not had to fight for space with lesser germs and had been free to grow unrestrained. They had become immune to the existing medicines of the time, causing illness and infections which led to serious cases of septicaemia. Scientists were now fighting to discover new ways to fight these infections. The use of antibacterial substances was carefully monitored.

As he walked through the brightly lit corridors, Max could actually feel his heart beating inside his chest. It felt as though he had run there and he wondered if he was going to be ill. He grinned to himself; at least he was in the right place. There were very few people, being near the end of the times permitted for visiting. Most people seemed to be leaving, strolling towards the exit. His feet sounded very loud on the hard bright floor. He sort of wished again that he had brought Lucy. The rational part of him knew that she would be a hindrance, would whine and want to know what was going to happen, which Max himself didn't know. But he realised that he would be braver if she was there, in some bizarre way, looking after her would make him less worried about himself.

He passed a desk with nurses talking in low voices, frowning and checking their computer records. They held them lightly in their hands, comparing results. He would quite like to be a nurse when he was old enough, a technical nurse, not one of the patient carers. He enjoyed science, thought that using the latest equipment all day would be very satisfying.

No one seemed to be watching him, he felt nicely anonymous. He really needed to find out which section his father was in. He needed access to one of the nurse's computers.

He passed a nurse in an office. He could see her through the glass panelled door as she worked at her desk. It was normal for hospital doors to have glass panels, privacy panels. They could be changed from clear to opaque with the touch of a button, depending on how much privacy was needed. They had something similar in their bathroom window at home, his mother nagged him constantly about forgetting to change it and all the neighbours being able to watch when he relieved himself. Like he would care about something like that.

An idea began to formulate in his mind. He paused, thought, then retraced his steps to the nurses' station. He watched for a moment, choosing which nurse looked the most stressed, the most impatient, had the least time to spare. Then he approached her, wearing his lost boy face.

"Excuse me, are you Nurse Donning?"

She looked up, frowning, harried. "No".

"Oh, sorry, is that her in the office?"

"No, that's Nurse Peters. Why?"

But Max had the information he needed and was already walking away, thanking her over his shoulder. She shrugged and continued with her work.

Max knocked on the door and opened it. He made his eyes as big as he could and spoke breathlessly, "Nurse Peters? You are wanted immediately in the entrance foyer. They have intercom issues, are having a code two emergency and asked me to tell you".

He jiggled up and down and looked nervous, which was not difficult, while copying the terminology he had heard on viewing

59

experiences, hoping it was realistic. The nurse sighed, this was frequently happening, the technology was still less reliable than a person. It looked like an emergency, she had better go. She nodded, wasting no time in walking past Max and down to towards the entrance.

As soon as she was gone, Max slipped into her office, touching the glass control button on the door as he did so, turning it to an opaque white. Better to not be seen he decided. He snatched up her computer. He was good with computers, one of the best in his sessions. As he had hoped, in her hurry she had left the account open, there was no need to have her bar code. He quickly found the menu, called up the patient lists and entered his father's code. There were footsteps outside the door, hurrying towards him. He froze, holding his breath, looking for ways to escape, hide, there were none. The footsteps continued, clicking past the door, growing fainter as they made their way up the corridor. Max breathed again, in and out, swallowed, looked back at the screen. The screen blinked for a moment, as if it too was swallowing, then told him which room, in which section of the hospital, he needed to go to.

He checked his own computer, calling up a map of the hospital. More footsteps approached, walking quickly, towards the room, pausing at the door. The door began to open.

There was a metal trolley. The top was littered with gadgets and instruments which Max did not recognise. Underneath was a cupboard. It was small, but big enough for Max to squeeze into. As the door to the room swung open, the door on the trolley was pulled quietly shut from the inside.

Max pulled his legs tightly to his body, holding his breath, straining to hear. The whole trolley was metal, cold and hard against his body, his curled spine grating uncomfortably against the back of his confined hiding place. There was something beneath

60

him, some handwritten notes and a pen which pushed cruelly into his side as he lay curled and cramped.

A second person entered the room. Max heard their footsteps, the greeting of the nurse, who sounded cross.

"Ah, you have come to collect the amphiboliser? I expected it to leave earlier."

"One of those days I'm afraid," said the man cheerfully. Max felt the trolley begin to move. He was holding the door to the cupboard, a cabinet really, shut from the inside, fearful that it might swing open and reveal him. There was no handle; he had to use his fingers, curling them around the edge of the door, hoping they wouldn't be seen.

The trolley rolled across the smooth floor. If the man pushing it noticed the extra weight, he did not comment. Max could see nothing, only a slither of light seeping in through the almost shut door. He could feel that he was moving, felt slightly sick as the wheels whirred along, wondered where he was going. He felt each corner, heard the man greet colleagues as he met them in the corridor, a pause, then forward into a lift. Heard the doors hiss shut, the beep of a button pressed, the sensation of moving upwards. More forward motion, then a pause at a security point, the squeak of acceptance as a bar code was checked, the hiss of doors sliding open, more rolling.

Max's legs began to hurt. They were unused to being so cramped, so tightly confined and the muscles began to scream in protest. The finger holding the door shut was turning numb and ached. He bit down on his lip, determined to not move, not be discovered, sure he would be able to escape later.

Then another person, the rustle of clothes as they stood very close to the door. Low voices, Max could not decipher the words but it sounded like instructions. More rolling. Then another pause.

61

"Before you go, come and look at this. Oh, and you can take the linen basket with you when you leave. They didn't collect it this morning." The voices moved away, grew fainter. The hiss of another door opening, fading footsteps, the door closed.

Max waited. He strained to hear. Silence. He decided he was alone, began to move, impatient to be free, but still cautious. Slowly, slowly, releasing his aching legs, uncurling his locked fingers, gradually pushing open the door, waiting for shouts that never came, peering round.

There was no movement. There was the hum of a motor, the hiss and gurgle of a machine, but no people. Max inched from his hiding place. The pain in his legs was immense as the blood rushed back. He felt slightly dizzy, held onto the trolley for a moment, waited for his body to readjust, to recover from being folded so tightly.

There was a glass wall, beyond it a guard, standing with his back towards Max. It was rare for human guards to be used. Max recognised the national uniform from news bulletins, though had never before seen one in person. The guard stood facing a door, legs slightly apart, ready for action. He was facing a door, which Max guessed must lead out to the main corridor, the one he had been pushed along. No escape route that way. If the guard turned around, he would see Max.

Max turned to look around the section of room where he stood, the part separated by the glass wall. He kept his movements slow, not sure if he would cast shadows that might cause the guard to turn. He hoped there were no motion or heat sensors. Whatever was in this room was important, of high enough value for a human guard to be used. Human guards carried live ammunition - they killed people.

He was standing in a room with three beds. Each one was covered in a plastic tent, tubes snaking into them, wires sliding out.

At first Max worried he might be in a bacteria ward, may catch some deadly disease. He peered into the nearest bed, then stopped.

He knew that face. Had seen it many times. It was Midra, the main spokesperson on the Global Council. His face often appeared in debates, explaining new laws, on news programmes. That explained the human guard. Yet, it wasn't him, it wasn't Midra. Or was it?

Max bent closer. The same but not the same. No, he decided, it was not him, was too young. He knew that Midra was old, very old. He seemed to have been leading the Council for generations. Max had heard his father talk about laws that Midra had introduced when he was young, so this could not be him. It looked like him though. Very like him. Max supposed it was a much younger brother, weirdly similar in appearance, clearly very ill. He crept to the next bed, knowing he should leave but curious as to who might be allowed to share a room with the relative of someone so powerful.

He stopped, frowned. This too was Midra. Except it wasn't. Again. This person was even younger than the first, about the age of his own father, but with the features of the ancient Midra. Did all his relatives look identical?

The last bed seemed to be calling to him and he went over, had to see, to check if this was yet another identical relative. It was, but much younger, a boy. It could be the son of the man, the grandson of the Council leader. Yet the similarities were too similar, there was something too perfect about the copy, the imprint of features.

They did not look ill, despite lying motionless surrounded by instruments and tubes. Their complexions were healthy, their eyes peacefully shut as though taking a nap. Max was intrigued. Were the relatives of the great leader being kept in a coma for some reason? The white sheets were pulled up to their chests, which rose and fell in time with the whir and hiss of a machine. It seemed to

63

be breathing for them. Their arms rested peacefully on the cover, tubes attached to their forearms, sliding under the covers, up into their mouths.

Max was fascinated. He also needed to escape. He looked around.

The three beds were in the centre of the room, surrounded by machines and medical equipment. There was a computer attached to the far wall. No windows, and the only door, through the glass wall, led to wherever the people talking had gone, past the guard who might turn at any moment. There was also a large yellow container in the corner. It was that, or back into the cabinet he'd arrived in. Max checked the yellow hamper and as expected, it was full of linen. It was probably the linen he'd heard discussed, which meant it would be leaving with the porter. The metal cabinet might be staying for several days. He would fit inside, could hide under the sheets, hope the porter would remove them from the room, take them somewhere less secure.

Max climbed inside. This was far from easy as the wheels kept sliding and the edge was too high to step over. He worried that he would make a sound, the movement might be seen, some flicker that would cause the guard to turn. But he managed it, a final leap, a scrabble for the edge, a plummet into linen; then he settled down, pulled the sheets over his head, hoped the three sleeping relatives did not have a contagious disease. He waited.

It was hot under the sheets. Max wanted to adjust them but feared he would be seen. They smelt of chemicals, cleansing agents and something acidic. He had pulled them so they covered his face, except for a tiny gap where his nose would go. He did not want to suffocate. He waited. He could feel the tension in his muscles, his throat was dry and his head ached. He thought of nothing, all his senses straining to hear, waiting, waiting, waiting.

After an age, he heard voices, laughing, coming nearer. Then he felt movement. He was being rolled away. He wondered to where.

The yellow container rolled noisily along the floor. One of the wheels was sticking and Max could tell the porter was having difficulty rounding the corners. The porter swore frequently and spun the container roughly from side to side. Max lost count of the corners, concentrating hard on not crying out as he was jolted, trying to keep his position as still as he could. His arms were pressed against the sides, bracing himself against the jolts, knowing he must not cause a bump, a change in movement that would be noticed. He was aware they entered another lift, was not sure if it was the same one. Felt himself descend, hoped that was a good sign.

Suddenly a thought occurred to Max. Did hospitals wash linen or did they burn it? Was there a risk of infection if bedding was washed and reused? Was his yellow container heading towards a giant incinerator? Would there be chance for him to leap out before he was consumed by flames? Should he give up now, reveal himself to the porter and take his chances? He felt drained of all energy, sure that he would be sick and very close to tears. His adventure was nothing less than a nightmare. He did not now feel brave, the hero on a mission. He felt like a little boy who had made a monumental mistake. He began to think about his mother, stopped himself before the tears began to flow. He must not give up now, must not think beyond the present, keeping still, waiting to see what would happen. He could do this. He could still escape, find his father, take him back to the island. One stage at a time, he reminded himself, focus on one stage at a time. He took a deep breath, now was not the time to panic.

He did not have to wait long. A final stretch of corridor, juddering over each tile, then a sudden crash as his container was thrust against another in a line next to the wall. Voices - the porter complaining that he had been required to deliver linen, not his job, anyone would think he was a bot, not a human with a brain. Muttering about unnecessary security, that now he was late for his own work, could the day get any worse? Footsteps fading.

Again Max waited until there was silence, though less patiently than before, the need to escape the container being urgent. He could hear a machine, smell detergent, which was reassuring. He rose from the yellow plastic, shrouded in white like a ghost rising from a grave. He peered out from within his veil. He was at one end of a long corridor. Two men were at the other end, heaving linen from a row of yellow carts. They were concentrating on their work, faces grim, shouting comments to each other as they plunged their arms into the trolleys, threw their bundles into a large heap, moved to the next trolley. Max swung his legs over the edge, lowered himself onto the floor, waited. When there was no sound, no voice shouting for him to stop, he gradually stood, faced away from the men, began to walk. His knees were shaking and his stomach was tight but he managed to walk, step after step, further from the men. He reached the end of the corridor, saw a sign, people walking around, public and workers intermingled. He was allowed on this corridor, he was safe.

No one paid him any attention as he strode quickly down the corridors, calling up a hospital plan on his computer and planning his route. He did not glance behind, did not check every corner, he could have been any relation visiting a patient slightly later than was normal. Only he was aware of his ragged breathing, knew his legs were shaking, that there were unfallen tears behind his eyes. He so wanted to be at home, but there was no going back now.

"The next stage," he told himself. "Now for the next stage."

He turned a corner, walked the length of yet another white corridor. He passed the entrance to a ward dealing with infections, many warnings written in red flashing lights, telling him not to enter unless he was wearing a visitor's suit, available on level three. He passed quickly holding his breath; he had heard about those places, how easily germs could pass between people, how patients were kept in individual plastic tents, quarantined from the staff and visitors while the staff fought to control the infection. He was glad his father was not in one of those wards. Hoped he had not just visited one himself. Decided he had not, no point in worrying unnecessarily. They would have sent a bot, he told himself, not a human porter, if there had been any risk of infection.

He slowed; he was nearing his father's section. The signs told him he was approaching neurology. *Neurology?* Why would his father be there? Nothing was wrong with his brain. He checked his map again, no, this was right. He began to count doors, looking for the correct number...Nearly there, nearly finished what he'd come to do.

It was an individual room, on his right, the door was closed but the glass in it was clear and he peered in. There was his father, sitting on the bed. His hair was cut very short and he appeared to be wearing pyjamas. Max found this disturbing, nightclothes made people look vulnerable, less capable somehow. Although he had known his father was a patient, he had expected him to be wearing clothes, to look like himself. He had hoped, on finding his father, that all the responsibility would be lifted, he would no longer be in charge, his father would take over. For the first time, he began to wonder if perhaps this had been unrealistic. Max began to question what he was doing, to wonder if it would even be possible. Too late now. No one else was in the room so he leant on the door, pushed it open.

His father turned, saw the boy, looked confused.

Then his face cleared, his eyes filled with tears and he crossed the room, engulfed Max in a hug that lasted a long, long minute.

"My son," he whispered into Max's hair, "my son".

The door opened behind them. Max withdrew, turned to see a nurse enter. She carried a small computer and a tray of implements. She paused very briefly then touched the glass button in the door, turning it opaque.

"Ah, the son," she said. "We have been expecting you."

The Nurse

Max was now alarmed. Why would they have been expecting him? How did they know anything about him? And why had she opaqued the glass, meaning that no one could see inside the room?

Max glanced at his father. His eyes were red with emotion, he had loosened his grip on Max but still rested his hand on his shoulder. It was very warm, very heavy. His father was not a man given to emotional expressions, he did not often hug Max, and Max had never seen him cry before. Ever. Max was aware that there was something weird happening, something which he had not suspected. His father did not look ill, other than wearing pyjamas, and having ridiculously short hair, so why was he in hospital?

People were rarely admitted to hospital unless surgery was necessary. Most illnesses could be diagnosed by the online doctor, using the health checking technology that every family kept safely in a drawer. They could monitor your heartbeat, your breathing, your temperature. Sometimes you needed to submit samples, and these tended to be couriered by the fleet of delivery services that swarmed around the town, bots and drones whisking packages to the hospital.

Of course, everyone did attend hospital once every year, for their annual health check. There was an exercise and health checking facility on level one. They watched you exercise, analysed the results, decided if you were eating correctly, exercising sufficiently. If you failed, were found to be under or overweight, then you received salary reduction until you were back to your estimated full health range. They took into account if you had an illness, something that could not be controlled, but every citizen was expected to take good care of their body, to not waste the global community's health resources through neglect or over indulgence. Keeping your body healthy was a duty, not an option.

Anyone who wanted to undertake something considered dangerous or risky to health had to first receive permission from the authorities. This rule covered everything, from using thrilling transportation considered unsafe (like water cycle drones) to smoking or inhaling substances to change mood. Very little was illegal, the Council did not ban dangerous activities, but nor would they finance the consequences. Individuals had to show that they owned sufficient funds to pay for any medical bills that arose, that they were able to take responsibility for any consequences. The Global Council was hot on citizens taking responsibility.

Max had already had his first independent medical, attending without a parent present. He had passed easily, felt rather proud of himself. Had he failed, his parent's salaries would have been reduced until a retest showed that he was at an expected fitness level. There would also have been restrictions on the food they could order, and Max's own entertainment choices would have been limited.

However, to be an actual patient was rare. Max did not like seeing his father so weak and he had no idea what the nurse had meant. She was busy now; unpacking her medical paraphernalia onto a trolley, there seemed to be a syringe involved. Max checked the door, estimated whether his body mass was sufficient to push past her if necessary, decided it probably was. He moved further from his father, freeing himself for a speedy exit. The nurse was now smiling. He did not trust her at all.

"You look worried, and there is not time to explain everything. Please listen for a moment, then you can decide what to do, I am not going to stop you leaving if that is what you want to do," she said, guessing his thoughts, reading his plans to flee in his wild-eyed glances towards the door. She moved away from it, leaving his pathway clear, hoping to calm him, alleviate some of his fears.

Max visibly relaxed a little.

She continued, "We were told you had left the island, and have been monitoring your movements. We wanted to keep you safe. We need you to help us move your father, it's very important for him to leave the hospital but it wouldn't be safe for one of us to take him.

"Do you think you could do that? Could you take him back to the island?"

While she spoke his father just stood there, listening, but blankly, as though the words made no sense to him. He kept looking at Max, smiling at him in a vacant, confused manner.

"What's wrong with him? Why is he here? And why is he wearing pyjamas?" asked Max.

The nurse smiled again. Max was unable to read her thoughts. She had slowed her speech, her body language was unthreatening. She looked as if she was being careful to not scare him away. He wondered if that made her more or less of a risk to his plan.

"There isn't time to explain everything, you can ask on the island, ask John to tell you. Your father has had his brain fiddled with, they tried to alter his thinking. It didn't work, it never does. But this time they want to try again, see if they can alter it using a different technique. We want to help him to leave before they can do that, before they cause more serious damage."

She saw the horror in the boy's eyes, quickly tried to reassure without lying. "He'll be alright, they just changed his memories. His brain will repair, it will find new pathways so he can think as well as he did before, but it will take time. He needs you now, needs you to help him. He will be very tired, thinking in a new way

70

uses a lot of energy. He is getting better, he's strong enough to travel, but he needs someone to help him with the thinking. Just until the brain has finished repairing. Can you do that? Can you take him safely to the island? They will help you when you get there, they can explain more." She glanced at the door. "I am worried someone might come, you really ought to leave."

"But he's in pyjamas," said Max. He could not take his father through the hospital wearing pyjamas. Everyone would stare. Someone might try to stop them, it wasn't normal behaviour. It would be embarrassing.

"Yes, you need to leave on your own. I cannot access your father's clothes, not without arousing suspicion. You need to go home now, come back tomorrow during visiting hours. Bring some of your father's clothes. Can you do that or do you want me to send you a list?"

"Come back again? To the hospital?" Max had had enough of the hospital. He wanted to leave and never return. He certainly didn't want to have to repeat the trip tomorrow. He began to search for excuses.

"And can he walk far? The island is a really long way," Max said, not sure if this was possible. Now that he was here, now someone was actually asking him to do what he had always intended to do, he felt himself resisting. He didn't feel in charge anymore.

"There is nothing wrong with your father physically, other than he will get tired so you might need to stop for rests." She looked at the door again.

"You really do need to go now. I am worried they will find you here. Come back tomorrow. At ten o'clock, I can be here then." She sounded worried, desperate even.

Max didn't understand, but neither did he feel he had any option. He nodded and moved towards the door. Perhaps he would think of a better plan later, when everything was less of a rush, when he'd had time to recover.

"Well done," whispered the nurse as he walked past her, "you are a star".

Then in one fluid movement, she lifted her computer, took a reading of his bar code.

"Check your messages later," she instructed. As Max left she turned the glass back to clear and began to busy herself with the syringe.

#

Max walked quickly away from the room. He felt light headed and slightly sick and very out of control. This was not at all what he had expected. He had planned to have a proper talk with his father, find out when he would be well enough to travel, explain about his mother and the island. Instead he had spoken only to a nurse, a stranger. One who seemed to know a lot about him. Who knew about the island, about John. As he walked, the worries drummed through his mind, keeping time with the rhythm of his footsteps on the hard white floor. Were they trapped in some dangerous web? Exactly who was involved? Did his mother have the first idea what was going on or had she naively led them all into danger?

Max passed the nurse's desk, they were still there, discussing their computer records. They paid no heed to him as he hurried past. He arrived at the entrance, realised he had not ordered a car to take him home, realised he was hungry. He sent a message for a car and found a food dispensing machine near the exit. He sat on a plastic sofa within sight of the pickup point, munching something covered in chocolate and something salty. They tasted old but he did not much care, the action of eating was comforting, helped him to feel in control, a little less like crying. He knew they were expensive; anything containing sugar was very expensive, reserved for treats and emergencies. This came into the latter category.

When Max arrived home the man watched him leave the car, unlock the door, hurry inside. He made no move, merely registered the facts in his computer, kept everyone informed. He watched the windows light up as the boy moved around the house, the hallway, the kitchen, up the stairs then down again, into the garden. That was surprising. But not important. As long as the boy did not leave the house again his instructions were clear, he was to remain where he was. He shuffled in his seat, watching the remote feed from the camera on the tree outside the boy's house. It was mostly boring.

#

Max stood in the garden, looking up at the yellow sky. He felt suddenly very young, very small, very alone. Today had been too difficult. He had managed, he had found his father, not been caught. But he felt exhausted, as if something inside had been used up, weakened. He wasn't sure he could be brave anymore, wasn't sure he could bear to return to the hospital tomorrow.

The garden was peaceful. It was tiny, but everyone had some kind of growing space, somewhere to plant things. It was considered healthy. His mother had planted theirs and the fronds of delicate leaves reached towards him, as though offering to hug him. It smelt green. Damp soil and humid air. There were great pots of flowering shrubs, baskets hanging from hooks with trailing leaves. He had never listened when his mother had told him their names, hardly even noticed them before. Now they felt very alive, an uncomplicated life form that didn't threaten him, they seemed comforting.

Nearby he could hear water, he knew the people three units away had a small fountain in their growing space, and he stood and listened to the cascade of water as the tears streamed down his cheeks. He was very tired, he did not want to do this, it was too big for him. A great lump of fear and loneliness welled up from his chest, sliding down his cheeks as fat wet tears.

Then he wiped his face on his hands, sniffed loudly and went back inside. That was enough.

He went to find some clothes for his father and began to stuff them into a backpack. Shirt, sweater, trousers, underwear (bit odd to touch your parent's underwear) shoes. The backpack was too small. He went into the basement, found a larger bag, stuffed the clothes inside. He rolled it to the kitchen. Added food and drink. Now it was too heavy to be comfortable but there was nothing he could do about that. He knew they were working on the technology to produce a bag with an air jet button in the handle, so when you reached terrain unsuitable for rolling, you could float the bag, it could hover over bumps and up steps. But that was for the future, Max wished it was available now but it was not. He heaved the bag to the front door and left it there, like a dog on sentry duty.

Eventually, Max went to bed. The empty house was filled with sounds, people moving around, monsters filling the dark corners, someone coming to find him. He kept the light on and a viewing experience flickered across his ceiling, distracting him, letting his mind wander. When he slept it was fitfully, full of dreams where people walked who had no brains, their bodies empty shells, living in white rooms with harsh lights. He did not see the light on his computer flash, telling him he had a message. He did not hear the cars that passed in the night. He slept the sleep of an exhausted boy.

Chapter Four

Discharged

When Max woke the sun was streaming through the cracks in his black out curtains, reaching out to find a way inside, piercing holes through the darkness. He pressed the 'open' button from his bed and shielded his face as the sunlight rushed in, bruising his eyes. For a moment, he forgot why he was there, assumed his parents were in the house with him, Lucy in her room across the hall. Then he remembered the island, and his father in the hospital, and the heavy knot came back into his stomach.

He reached for his computer, saw he had messages. They were all from the nurse. There was a list of clothes his father would need, like Max was too stupid to do that on his own. There was a reminder to meet her at 10 o'clock. He glanced at the time, no need to hurry.

There was also a certified report, for which Max was suddenly grateful. It was backdated, and verified that Max had been absent from both school sessions and learning experiences due to ill health. He would be well enough to recommence learning next week, though would continue to be absent from school sessions. This was a huge help. A copy had been logged with the central computer. Things went astray all the time, they would assume the delay was either human error or technological malfunction but no one would question its validity. It meant two things. Firstly, Max could legitimately use his own bar code, he had a reason for having not studied, no one would try to trace him. Secondly, most importantly, it meant he could continue his learning on the island. He would have his computer with him.

He should probably take his sister's computer too. He swung out of bed, used the bathroom then plodded across to his sister's room. Pink and white. Seemed completely unnecessary to him for

75

girls to be quite so girly. Even her spare computer was pink. He found it in a drawer, under a heap of beads and bracelets. His image watched him from a dozen mirrors around the walls. It was weird, like being in a room of himself multiplied many times. As a whim he grabbed one of her toys, a rabbit, its fur almost completely worn away, the limbs hanging limply where the stuffing had compacted. It was one of her favourites. She was annoying, but she would like to have it. He stuffed it into the bag, next to one of his father's shoes. Then he went in search of food, feeling like a hero. Nothing more he could do until he had eaten.

Max dug into the freezer and pulled out some bacon panini sandwiches. They were hard as stone and the cold numbed his fingers. He put two in the microwave and set the time, returned the others to the freezer and slammed the door, hearing his mother's voice in his head telling him to close it gently. He put his mouth under the juice tap (another banned activity) and took a swallow. It tasted bitter after cleaning his teeth and he spat it into the sink. He looked at the splattered yellow droplets for a moment, then sluiced them away. He took a mouthful from the water tap instead. Much better. He forced it between his teeth, puffing out his cheeks, rinsing his mouth. Then he reached for a glass and filled it.

The water on the island tasted weird, he did not like it all (there was not much on the island that he did like.) He had asked Agnes about it and she said that it came from a well, was pumped straight to their tap with nothing added. Max was not sure if that was legal, but maybe laws were different if you did not live on the mainland. Here they added all sorts of things to the water, stuff to clean your teeth, vitamins and a low dose of hormones. He knew (from science sessions) that the hormones were to eliminate unwanted pregnancies but had also helped to make males generally less inclined to fight.

If a couple wanted to have a child, they had to apply for permission to drink bottled water, which arrived in large vats every week. Max had seen them being delivered to other houses and his mother had explained what they were. The authorities first checked your health status, ensuring you did not carry any inherited defects. They also checked your income, to ensure you were able to support a child. You had to pay quite a large tax, which increased drastically with each child you had, before you were allowed the hormone-free water. Apparently this also helped to improve the general intelligence of the population, as only high intellect professions were paid well. People with lower intelligence had jobs which were less well paid, so they couldn't afford to have children. The Global Council valued intelligence.

There were no set rules on how many children a couple could have if they were both healthy and financially sound, but most families only had one or two children. Many had none, preferring to travel or live in a better street or take a higher promotion. One parent had to agree to forego certain job levels when a couple had children, agreeing to input a certain amount of time and energy into raising them. In his own family, his mother had taken this role. Until her youngest child was aged sixteen, she would not be eligible to apply for any promotion that involved more time or responsibility. Some people, those who were already in senior positions when they decided to have children, were actually required to take a demotion. The Global Council only granted parenting permission to those people willing to make these sacrifices.

Max had a friend who was the third child in his family and he said it was annoying, the best cars only carried up to four passengers, they always had to order the cheaper ones. Three children was unusual. As the more senior positions at work were held by childless couples, this was seen by many to be a desirable state. The population was naturally decreasing.

Max finished drinking and prepared to leave.

By 10 o'clock, Max was back at the hospital and walked slowly back towards his father's room. The brightness of the harsh overhead lighting was annoying, uncomfortable on his eyes. The bag was heavy and as he pulled it along the floor he could hear the wheels grinding. There were lots of people, all hurrying to visit relatives or be on time for appointments. The staff bustled around in their white uniforms, holding computers or medical equipment, looking cross. He passed the infections ward, saw suited relatives like men from outer space going in to see their loved ones. The outfits rustled as they walked, looked clumsy and uncomfortable. But at least they were protected from germs.

As he neared his father's room, Max slowed. He felt uneasy about this, there was something he did not understand, something that felt wrong. He knew nothing about this nurse but had obeyed her instructions without question; perhaps he was as naive as his mother. Or as desperate. He reached the doorway and peered round, tensed to flee if he saw anything untoward, anything that seemed like a trap.

His father was sitting on the bed. He still wore his pyjamas, still had bare feet. The nurse was there. No one else. The nurse stood to one side, checking something on her computer, not looking at his father, not speaking, absorbed in what she was doing. Max considered whether he could get his father out without her seeing, decided it was impossible, he would have to trust her. He entered the room.

She looked up and smiled as he went in.

"You are on time, well done. Did you manage to collect his clothes okay?" she asked, as if it was a difficult task, as if he were a young child. Max nodded.

His father looked up, smiled.

"Hello son," he said, as if he had been expecting him. Perhaps he was less confused than Max had thought. At least he seemed less emotional today.

Max unloaded the clothes onto the bed and his father started to dress. Max turned away slightly, uncomfortable with his father's nudity. The nurse began to give him instructions.

"You should go straight to the island, don't go back to your own house. I can change your father's records temporarily, showing him as discharged, but when the next nurse arrives she will probably cancel that and they will start to search for him. When you are on the island we think he will be safe, it will be too noticeable to get him back and the authorities would rather not advertise some things. They will accept he has gone, and as long as he does not try to make a fuss, to cause any trouble, they will be happy for him to go. At least, we hope so…" she paused.

Max wondered what she was talking about, it made no sense to him. But he understood that he needed to get his father to the island, which had been his plan all along, so he let her talk.

"Don't go back to the guesthouse. It is not the best route now. There is another tunnel; it joins the one you used. You can enter it in the designated holy building in the town. You can't miss it, it is right in the centre of the old part of town, not far from the cliff. It used to be a church and it has a tall tower, which you can see from miles away. I have sent the address to your computer so you can program the car. When you get there, go to the back of the hall, as though you are going to climb the tower. Instead, go through the small green door on your left. It will be unlocked. You will find steps leading down. If you follow them, they will take you to the tunnel.

"It would be best to not leave your father alone at all until you are at the island. He might be confused and wander off. You will also find that he gets very tired, especially after he has used his brain, watching things, listening to something, things like that. Not so much physical things, so the walk should be fine but the journey there will tire him, lots of visual stimuli, even though he will just be sitting. Remember, it is his brain that needs time to heal, not his body. Anything that uses his brain will exhaust him. Let him rest, have a nap if necessary. He is strong enough though, so don't worry."

Max was frowning, he was not sure how difficult this would be, not sure if his father was up to it. What exactly had they done to him? The nurse was still speaking but he interrupted her.

"What's wrong with his brain? Will he be alright?"

"Yes, yes," she reassured him quickly, glancing at the time. "His memories will be a bit off, that's all. Plus the tiredness. He'll mend."

"What memory things?" asked Max, worried. "Will he remember my mum and sister? Does he know who he is?" He looked at his father who was dressed now and was sitting on the bed. He looked confused and was holding his shoes, one in each hand. His feet were bare.

"Oh, I may have forgotten socks!" said Max and felt giggles bubbling up inside.

"Never mind, he'll have to wear just shoes, there's no time now," said the nurse.

"His long term memory is fine. More than fine. You'll find out about that, ask John. No, it's short term stuff, you might have to say things twice, things like that." She was moving towards the door, trying to hurry them, usher them out.

Max's father pushed his pyjamas into the bag, then looked confused.

"Will I need these?" he asked his son.

"You might," said Max, who also wanted to leave now. "Come on Dad, let's get a move on."

His father attached his bar code to his sweater, then lifted the suitcase easily and turned to the nurse. He didn't seem able to hurry, each action was very deliberate, one thing done at a time, as if it needed all his thinking capacity to do that one action.

"Thank you. For everything," he said to her. Then he followed Max out of the door.

Max was walking quickly. He felt in control again, he knew what he needed to do. He slowed his pace when he realised his father wasn't keeping up, not sure if he could tell him to hurry. As he walked he was checking his messages, entering the code the nurse had sent to the car order, using his mother's bar code to pay. No one looked at them as they left. They could have been anyone, a boy and his father leaving hospital, carrying a case – maybe one of them had been a patient, maybe they had been delivering items for someone else. Max felt safely anonymous as they approached the waiting bay, walked under the flow of safe bacteria, found the car Max had ordered with its number flashing on the roof. They climbed inside and Max checked the internal camera was off, checked the destination code was the one the nurse had given him, strapped himself in. His father was gazing out of the window, watching people arrive. The bag was stowed on the back seat. The car moved away.

#

Neither man nor boy noticed the man watching them from the entrance foyer. Nor did they see him enter the car number into his computer and press send.

A New Entrance

The car moved away from the hospital. Max was fiddling with the bag, wondering if he had brought enough food. He was hungry, could do with a snack now but probably he should wait. He was feeling better now, more like his old self. Things had become exciting again, rather than scary, and it looked like his plan was working. He had rescued his father, done what he came for.

His father watched him. It was so good to see him again. He felt as if he had been in the hospital for an age, had lost all trace of time. Walking had felt strange, it was a while since he had done any. It was nice to move again, to leave that room, to not wonder who was about to enter, with food or an injection or a move to a treatment room. Nice to feel some control seeping back, to feel human again, to be a person not a patient. He felt slow, fuzzy, as if he was slightly drunk. He had been told that would pass, his mind would eventually clear again. He hoped so. He understood everything, knew what was happening, but speaking was an effort, he could form the words but actually saying them was difficult, as if there was a link missing. Luckily no one seemed to be expecting much conversation, Max seemed lost in his own thoughts.

The car moved almost silently, a gentle purr, for which the father was grateful. There was something wrong with his ears. His ears or his brain, he was not sure which. All sound caused a vibration, it was uncomfortable. When people spoke it sounded as though their voice was computer generated, like a machine talking through a voice box. It was unpleasant and he was glad that his son was silent, fiddling with the bag and looking out of the window.

He turned and watched the houses and buildings as they passed. Roads lined with trees, houses nestling together, the solar panels used for emergency power glinting as they faced the sunlight, each tile mounted so that it could swivel to follow the path of the sun throughout the day. Meeting places, lined with benches that were sheltered from the weather, areas of grass where people could meet, chat, children could play, practice sports. They were passed by a luxury car, fashioned like one from centuries before, a long bonnet, a low roof, tinted glass in the windows hiding the occupant.

Their own car slowed, allowing other traffic to pass. They were level with the old school and memories flooded back – arriving in the school bus, jostling with the other boys as they fought to get off, their bags snagging on the seats and each other. Walking up the driveway, fearing detention because his homework was not completed. The smell of the corridors, the hard plastic seats, the sarcastic teachers standing in front of black boards.

"I remember going there," he said, "I hated it. Always seemed to be in trouble for something". He laughed, remembering.

Max looked at him for a long moment. When he spoke it was slowly, as if to a child.

"What do you mean Dad? When did you visit there? It hasn't been a school for centuries, about two hundred years I think."

His father frowned, confused. He could see that what the boy said was correct, could tell from the age of the bricks, the renovations that were looking dated themselves, that it was an historical site, preserved but not functioning, had not functioned for many many years, possibly centuries. Yet he remembered. He could have told Max which classes where taught behind each window, the name of the head teacher and what they called him behind his back, who his friends were, who used to wait by the corner where the school office was and try to trip people up as they passed. He knew the smell of the locker room where they hung damp coats and rummaged through wooden cubbyholes searching for books. Yes, books, pages folded in the corners, ink seeping through from where his pen had leaked, heavy hardback science manuals and thin paperback novels. Reams of paper trapped in plastic folders with rings that snapped shut. He remembered. He remembered as clearly as if it were yesterday.

Which was clearly impossible because he also remembered his remote learning as a boy, the lessons online, the occasional school sessions in a stuffy room with a teacher when they had already understood everything from the computer tutor. The two memories did not tally, and yet each was there. Each was real. He frowned and was silent. He could not explain it to the boy, feared he might be going mad, though felt sane. It made him feel insecure, vulnerable. If you could not trust your own brain, what did you have as a point of reference, what could you trust?

The car had moved past the school now and was gathering speed as it left town and joined one of the main arteries eastwards.

"Are you hungry?" asked the boy, pulling out some crackers. The father shook his head, still reluctant to speak, wanting to avoid those strange echoing vibrations in his head. He wanted to ask how his wife and daughter were, to explain to the boy what had happened to him. But it was too uncomfortable, and the effort of forcing words out was too tiring. Instead he merely smiled, gazed out of the window as the scenery whizzed past.

Max munched his way through a packet of crackers and some cheese. The cheese was hard, had possibly been in the fridge for too long. He was worried about his father, wondering why he had said that strange thing outside of the school. He could tell it had worried his father too, had noticed the look of panic in his eyes when he realised that he was talking nonsense. Max was not sure how well he was going to cope if his father was now insane. He needed him to help, to sort out the sleeping arrangements, to tell his mother that Max needed to continue with his school sessions and his contact with his friends. He would like to start discussing that now really but probably it was inappropriate, probably he should wait for a while, until his father looked less tired. He could do that, he was not a completely self-absorbed child, he could behave like an adult, bide his time.

The car slowed again as it entered another town. Max looked at his father. He had fallen asleep. Probably for the best, they had a long walk ahead. He looked at the houses as the car followed the main roadway down a hill which curved between buildings. Old towns were always like that, the older the place the more twisted the roads. There had been plans once to demolish great swathes of building and re-plan towns with straight roads, like the grid system that some other countries had adopted. Of course, too many people objected, no one wanted to lose their house and the historians had hurriedly put preservation orders on too many buildings to make it practical. That was the trouble with England, it was too proud of its history, too unwilling to destroy things for the sake of improvement.

Max could see the holy place from the very edge of the town. Just as the nurse had said, the tower could be clearly seen from a long way back, growing ever taller as they wound their way towards it. When they eventually reached it, it seemed less tall than Max had expected and he realised that some of the perceived height was because it was set on a slight hill in the centre of town.

The car stopped next to a low wall surrounding the garden area of the holy place. Once it had probably been a graveyard around a church but the graves would have been cleared long ago, the remains cremated and disposed of. Now it was a garden, filled with trees and flowers, with a stone path leading to the arched entrance.

Max shook his father awake.

"Dad, we're here, we're at the holy place that nurse sent us to. Are you alright? Can you walk? Can you carry the case?"

His father nodded, climbed out of the car, lifted the case and put it on the path next to him. He stretched, enjoying the feel of the midday sun on his face, the tug of the wind at his clothes. It was so nice to be free from the hospital, to feel weather again, to see colour. The hospital had been very white. He felt hungry for colour. He followed his son into the building, through the wooden side door and into the main sanctuary.

Their eyes took a moment to adjust to the gloomy interior of the large space inside. There were stone pillars holding up the arched roof, the beams centuries old, wooden, and beginning to crumble in places. Max could see the signs that showed it was constantly being renovated, nearly matching shades of paint, the odd wooden beam not blackened with age. He guessed it was one of the town's treasures, there would not be any suggestion that it might be allowed to fall into decay. It smelt of dust and old wood and was filled with pews, covered in multi-coloured cushions, all facing forwards. The front was a series of arches, the central one had a pulpit for the speaker to stand in and a large blank screen, where visual aids could be programmed. There was a raised section beyond, Max guessed that musicians and choirs would perform there, adding mood to the services.

Around the walls were symbols from most of the major religions. Max had learnt them all during school sessions, had been taught that it was important to respect all beliefs, that none was more important, more right, than any other. This had been strongly denied in the privacy of his own home, his father had frequently, strenuously, fought to uphold his own faith over all others. But there was no place for such unrelenting belief in today's society. It was divisive, in a world that valued unity.

They stood together for a moment, man and boy, gazing at the symbols on the walls. There was the curved Omkar symbol, looking almost like numbers, representing the three elements of the Hindu Om: Brahma Shakti the creator, Vishnu Shakti the preserver, and Shiva Shakti, the liberator. There was also the Hindu swastika carved into the pillar next to it.

On the next pillar was the Islam star and crescent and the word for Allah written in curvy script. Beyond that was the Star of David and there was a seven-branched candlestick, the menorah, standing on a table at the front. Islamic and Jewish symbols were often placed together, as they were considered religions so similar they almost blended into one.

There was an image of Deg Tegh Fateh and the symbol of Khand, showing the sword, chakkar and kirpans that were important to the Sikh religion.

Next to them, painted in heavy black paint onto the stone wall was an imposing Torii gate, marking the entrance to the spirit world for those following Shinto. Next to that, nearer to them, was the black and white Taiji, the Yin and Yang of Taoism. Right beside them was the Buddhist Wheel of the Dharma and a lotus flower of purity.

In the corner was the pentagram of Wicca. Next to it was the nine pointed star of Baha'i.

Beyond that, on the far side, was the Christian cross, made from wood and fixed to the wall opposite the door. It looked new, and Max wondered what had happened to all the Christian symbols that must have originally festooned the walls. Only one stained glass window remained, the light filtering through images of Jesus and disciples.

Max had come to one of these holy places a few times, had sat with his parents and sister. Most people chose to sit near the symbol that represented their own religion but Max had been told that it did not matter, that they believed that God surrounded them, that emblems were of little significance. Max was not sure what he himself believed. He rather liked the holy places, with their eclectic mix of symbols, places where people could go and celebrate all the festivals that they had enjoyed for centuries, could listen to an interesting lecture given by a different religious leader in turn, each one careful to not say anything that might be offensive to another religion, all talking about peace, unity, being generous and kind. Things that no one would dispute, would deny were important.

They had not attended recently though. Max's father had held secret meetings in their home for the last few years. Max and Lucy knew that these were not allowed, had been declared unhealthy by the Council. They did not discuss them with friends or at school sessions. Max's father was a music tutor, it was not unusual for a variety of people to enter their home, to receive tuition on an instrument. It was thought that those in authority either did not know or did not care that they were holding religious meetings, gatherings where it was stated there was only one God, that only the Bible was a holy book. Saying things that were banned, considered divisive and unhealthy for society.

They turned away from the symbols on the walls and walked to the Wheel of the Dharma. The floor was raised slightly at the rear of the church, with a stone walkway leading to the very back. The lotus flower was etched into a wooden door. They turned the ancient latch and found themselves in a small hallway. To one side was a notice, advising them that it was permissible to climb the tower, there were one hundred and seventy-one steps and that there was no elevator, so they needed to be capable of walking both up and down. The Global Council would take no responsibility for the health of anyone taken ill during the climb. There were stone steps leading up, winding round and round a central pillar, each step dipped slightly in the centre where a million feet had worn it away.

On their left was a small green door. It was unlocked, and ignoring the 'Private' sign they pushed it open. There were more steps, this time leading downwards. They looked at each other for a moment, then Max led the way down.

#

After they had gone, the old woman waited for five minutes. Then she rose from her place kneeling beside the cross, hidden from view by the tall backed pews. Her knees were stiff and she rested for a moment, leaning against the pillar that had the pentagram etched into it, before moving to the back of the church. In her hand she carried a large metal key and she used it to lock the small green door. Then she pulled her phone from her pocket and ordered a car to take her home. She was a link in a chain. Her job was done.

Chapter Five

Back on the Island

Max woke. He could hear Lucy's breath coming in little snorts. She would probably snore when she was older. The floor pressed up into his shoulders and he wriggled on his heap of blankets. Uncomfortable. This was so not what he had planned. He had thought that when his father was here, matters would improve, the adults would realise how inappropriate it was for him to be sharing a room with his little sister. So far, nothing had changed, nothing had happened as he had expected.

He had walked with his father through the tunnel, finding where it joined the route from the guesthouse, continuing on to the beach. They had stopped once so his father could rest and Max could eat something. They had sat in the dark on the cold rock, leaning against the tunnel wall. It was not comfortable, but it allowed his legs a break. His father had ripped strips from his old pyjamas, used them to pad his shoes slightly, to stop them rubbing against his bare feet. Max felt a bit embarrassed about that, about forgetting socks, but there had been a lot to do, a lot to think about, with his mother not being available to provide food and things.

His father had not spoken much on the journey, had seemed unperturbed by the dark, happier almost. Max had felt happier too, there was nothing scary when he walked with his father. The tunnel had seemed shorter on the return trip.

When they arrived at the beach, his mother was there to meet them. She had been kept informed by John, knew everything that had happened, almost been part of the plan. She hugged Max long and hard, he saw tears in her eyes, but she said very little, told him he was brave, she was glad he was safe. Lucy seemed to think he was a hero, squealed when she saw the toy he had brought, looked at him with big adoring eyes. That wouldn't last long. John told him well done, he had been a huge help, done a good job.

Only Agnes had held back. She had told him she was pleased he was safely back, cooked him a huge dinner, smiled. But there was something in her eyes behind that smile, a hardness that told Max that she wasn't fooled, she knew his motives weren't all good, was angry at the deception, she would discuss it with him later. He would have to avoid being alone with her for a bit, until she forgot about it. He didn't need a lecture, another adult telling him what he'd done wrong.

He arched his back, stiff from another night on the floor. His parents were in John and Agnes' room. The old couple had insisted, said it was only right, they would be honoured if his father would take their room, especially as he wasn't well. They would sleep in the lounge, possibly share a friend's house if it became too uncomfortable. That left one bed free in the spare room, which everyone else seemed to think should belong to Lucy, despite her being younger, having done nothing to save their father, just being a girl was enough, apparently. Hardly fair.

His father had slept almost as soon as they finished their meal, quietly excusing himself and slipping from the room. John had said he would explain some things to him today, after he had rested. Max hoped he would be allowed to hear too, there was a lot he didn't understand.

He knew now that most of his trip had been monitored, with reports sent back to the island, which would explain why his mother had not been completely insane with worry. Apparently John's grandson now owned the guesthouse, he had known Max was arriving, had told them he was safe. There seemed to be a whole network of people on the mainland, all working to help people escape to the island. John called them the Watchers. Max did not know why. Nor did he know where the rescued people went to next. This worried him. He would talk to his father about it. When he was well enough, when he no longer said strange things about having impossible memories. When he appeared sane again.

While Max was getting dressed upstairs, his father was in the kitchen. Agnes was pouring tea from a large brown pot while he spread butter on thick toast. The knife scraped the surface, reminding him of something, something to do with boats. A fleeting memory that never quite surfaced before it slipped away. That was happening a lot and it worried him. Agnes saw his frown. She reached out a wrinkled hand, the fingers hardened by years of work.

"Try not to worry, it will all get easier. You have done so well, the hardest bit is over now. We'll get you back to strength, you'll soon find your feet again, you just need to go slowly, let everything heal."

He managed a weak smile. "The island seems a peaceful place to live," he began, "I stayed on an island once, when I was young. I remember my mother calling from the beach at mealtimes".

He remembered his mother calling him, shouting, "Dennis," above the cry of the wind. Then he remembered his father, calling him James when it was time to study. A teacher referring to him as Michael. The names crowded into his mind. Then another memory, his friend shouting a different name, telling him to hurry. Then signing documents, using yet another name, his name. But they were all his name.

He buried his head in his hands, ran his fingers through his newly grown hair, tugging at the roots, using the pain to remind him of what was real. It was all so confusing. He was going mad, perhaps already was mad. Nothing made sense, his head a jumble of impossible memories. He felt slightly queasy and pushed the toast away, appetite gone. He seemed to have been ill, not himself, for so long. Surely it was time now to be well again.

The door opened and John walked in, saw the man with his head bowed in despair, caught a long look from Agnes and strode into the kitchen. He took the tea Agnes offered but remained standing.

"John, I think Den is ready for some explanations," said Agnes, looking to her husband to make this right, to ease this man's agony.

He nodded. "Den, have you finished eating? Are you feeling well enough for a chat? I can explain some things to you. Perhaps help you to sort a few things." His tone was brisk, business like. It rallied Den. He took a breath, forced a smile.

"Yes, that would be good. Now would be good."

"Excellent, good man. Come along, we'll go into my office."

John led the way from the kitchen. In the hall they met Max who was hovering near the bottom of the stairs.

"Max, glad you're up nice and early. I am going to have a talk with your father, explain some things. I think perhaps you should come too. Do you want to? You can wait a bit longer for breakfast? Jolly good, come along then. We'll go into my study, we can be private in there." He touched the print reader to unlock the door and they filed inside.

The office was cool and tidy, a functional work place for someone busy. There was no clutter, simply technological aids on a large oak desk, chairs arranged next to a hearth with a single photograph frame above. A round rug softened the flagstone floor. There was something permanent about every room in the cottage, something well used, something that told you that many lives had passed through, your current visit was merely a glimpse in time. Max longed for the more temporary shine of the modern world.

John motioned for Den to sit in a high backed chair next to the empty fireplace. He pulled another chair from the desk for Max to sit on, then sat himself, on a low chair opposite them both. Max fiddled nervously with a button, wondering what he was about to hear, whether it would be true. Den sat still, staring blankly at the mantelpiece, watching pictures float across the photograph frame, the images powered by a tiny solar chip embedded in the frame. John leant forwards, resting his elbows on his knees, feet apart, eyes bright. Max thought he was the only one who looked relaxed.

"Now," said John, deciding to tackle the most complicated issue first, the one that was so frightening for people, "I believe you might have been remembering some strange events. You remember things that could not possibly be memories?"

Man and boy stared at him. Max was thinking of that strange incident outside the school when his father had claimed to be a student there. His father thought of all the weird things that kept floating through his mind. The multitude of names that he knew were his, the memories that were impossible, the madness that was fighting to take over. He nodded, like a wooden man with a stiff hinge. A simple single bow of the head, then that fixed gaze, willing John to speak, to explain.

John smiled, wanting to alleviate some of the tension.

"Well, first off, I don't think you are going mad, though I expect it feels a little like it. I think you are a rememberer. Have you heard of them?"

Max leaned forward. "That girl. The one who brought us here. You said she was a rememberer. I remember." He heard the strangeness of his sentence and giggled. He knew that he was correct, that when they had first arrived at the cottage, and his mother had mentioned the girl who showed them the island, who led them through the tunnel, John had called her a 'rememberer'. It was a strange term, sounded like something from a viewing experience.

"Yes, that's right, well done. She is. Her grandmother used to work in the guesthouse, when she was a girl. The girl who brought you here used those inherited memories to find the door to the tunnel." John had known the older woman for years. He had been no more than a child when the grandmother had worked at the guesthouse, when she herself was a girl, barely old enough to carry the heavy trays up to the dining rooms. She had lived in one of the attic rooms and had helped in the kitchen, serving meals in her neat black skirt and tiny white apron. She knew the house well. Later she had left, married and had children, then watched with pride when her grandchildren were born. One of them, the girl they were discussing, had joined the watchers, had revealed her special ability.

He glanced up, saw the man and boy looking at him. He saw their confusion, the disbelief in their eyes. There was no way to explain this quickly. He must try to order it better, to start somewhere near the beginning.

"In hospital, they tried to alter you, to change your brain so that you would stop believing and teaching that there is only one God. It threatens the Global Council, they need complete unity to function, complete authority. The idea of one God is unhelpful, so they try to remove that belief from your brain. We think that when they do that, they sometimes alter a different part of the brain, the memory part. It means that some people find that they can access memories that are dormant in the rest of us."

"But I can remember things that I never experienced," said Den, "things that cannot be memories".

"Not your memories no, not in the strictest definition of the word. They are inherited memories. Things that happened to your ancestors before they conceived the next generation, memories that were passed along." He waited, letting the idea sink in. Max frowned.

95

"That's impossible. Isn't it?" said Den, feeling it explained everything, knowing that logically it made no sense.

"It is not new science," said John, "but it still is not understood, not properly.

"Think of an animal, a bird perhaps. When it matures it makes a nest, how does it know how to do that? It lays eggs then keeps them at a constant temperature and humidity. How does it know? Then it raises the temperature by not leaving the nest around the time the hatchlings emerge. How does it know? Then it collects food, the right food for its own species and feeds the babies. How does it know? That is one form of inherited memory. We call it instinct. It goes beyond learned behaviour, beyond what can be acquired through watching adult birds.

"There were experiments, centuries ago, using mice. They were taught to fear a smell. This fear passed down to successive generations, even though they did not have the same experience. The next generation of mice was conceived in a test tube and never had any contact with their biological parents. So the fear of the smell was not copied behaviour. Yet when successive generations of mice, those who had never had contact with the original group, came into contact with the smell, they showed signs of fear. It is a form of genetic memory, sensory experience, an inherited fear.

"In humans, we think it is incorporated into the genome and explains phobias. Why are people afraid of heights? Maybe their grandfather fell off a ladder as a boy. Why are some people afraid of moths? Perhaps an ancestor had a frightening experience with winged creatures. We do not understand phobias, irrational fears that we know logically are silly. But we have them anyway. We are born with them. We have inherited them."

Max was nodding now. He picked up a pencil from the desk top and rolled it slowly under his hand, back and forth across the wooden surface while he thought. He hated spiders, always had.

He knew they couldn't hurt him, knew he was bigger, but they still freaked him out. He was interested by what John was telling them, perhaps there was a reason for his fear, perhaps he wasn't just a wimp.

John continued.

"I won't go into too much detail now, but there has been a lot of research over the centuries. Not so much recently. None that has been published anyway. Read some of Carl Jung's work, or some articles about Lamarckian inheritance. There is a transgenerational epigenetic inheritance that lies dormant within us. Things your ancestors experienced that caused chemical changes whilst not affecting the DNA code, things that got passed on.

"In most people they lie dormant, are never noticed other than perhaps a surprising phobia or a sudden intuition about something. But when they tried to alter your brain they changed part of your memory, your ability to recall things. Your short term memory will be damaged, you may not remember what you have just done, will forget names, have lost your sense of time, need people to repeat information. You will need to stay with your family for a while, try not to do too much, or go to new places where you might get lost. You also might find you are very emotional for a while, find things that would have affected you slightly in the past now move you to tears or anger more quickly."

Max found he was nodding again, glad that his father's odd moods were being explained rationally. He put the pencil back into the pot and grinned at his father. Now that was sorted, perhaps they could get back to normal.

John leaned even further forward, looked up into Den's eyes and spoke with quiet emphasis.

"But your long term memories, which are processed by the hippocampus, will have been stimulated. You will begin to access things you had forgotten. You will remember the memories of all your ancestors, everything stored in their brains up until they conceived the next generation. It is a tremendous ability. Your father, grandfather, great-grandfather. Your mother, grandmother, great-grandmother. Going further and further back, we don't yet know how far. You will remember their thoughts, their feelings, what they experienced."

Max was dreaming now, wishing he had the same ability. No need for all those awful mathematical school sessions, he would have inherited the memory of how to solve equations from his father or grandmother. He began to think about things that might be useful to inherit, to not have to do the hard work of actually learning them to be efficient. John was still speaking,

"At first those memories will be muddled, you will find it hard to tell which things were experienced by you and which are inherited. It will settle down though, the brain adjusts to amazing things. You will start to order your thoughts, will learn to access the information you want and to ignore the rest. It will all get easier, trust me."

"Trust me," thought Max, "that's the crux of the matter. Can we trust you?" Much of the science was too complicated, he had only half listened. He understood that his father's memory was changed though, that he now would remember things that his ancestors had experienced. It all sounded weird, he was not sure it was entirely a good thing. What if he remembered horrible things? If one of his ancestors had been a lunatic or a murderer? Nor was he completely convinced that it was true, though it did explain the odd things his father had said.

Den mainly looked relieved. He was not going mad after all. There was a reason for his crazy thoughts, it could all be explained. He sat for a moment, not trusting himself to speak, feeling that familiar rush of emotion that was now so hard to control, not wanting to cry in front of his son. But the relief, the beauty of knowing that it could be explained, that he was not just imagining everything.

John walked to the desk, tapped on the computer. He found some research for Den to read, something that would clarify what he had told him. He brought it up on the large screen and beckoned for Den to come and read it. He would give him some time, let the idea settle. Then they needed to decide what to do. Den could be useful to them now, perhaps the family leaving was not such a good idea. Perhaps they should send the mother and children ahead, persuade the father to stay. He would think about it some more, make his plan before he shared it. This needed careful thought.

More Discussions

Den stared at the computer. John had uploaded some material for him to read. It floated onto the screen, one word at a time, easily assimilated, no need for his eyes to scan from left to right. If he missed something, wanted to reread it, he could pause it, call the whole document onto the screen, go back to the part he had missed. He remembered when all documents were presented like this, whole pages of words rather than one at a time. And books, pages of lines of writing, his eyes traveling across each page, left to right, top to bottom. So much effort, so slow. Much faster to read articles or stories one word at a time, no eye movement involved. The speed the words appeared could be adjusted to suit the reader, as could font size and position. They lived in a world that was streamlined for the consumer. Everything was easy. On the surface. Den sighed, and began to read.

Max pulled his chair close and read over his father's shoulder. The words moved too quickly for him to keep up, many of them unfamiliar, written in the style of all ancient documents. He lost interest, sat back, looked around the room. He was interested by what John had told them, pleased to hear that his father was not insane, that his muddled memories would improve.

However, he was disappointed that this seemed to be the end of the explanation. He wanted to know more about the hospital, especially that strange room he had visited. It played on his mind, the images returning unbidden. Not that he could raise it. He was not sure how many rules and laws he had broken by being in there but he was sure his parents would be angry. Sure that he would be lectured, maybe even punished. He sighed. No, it was not something he could raise himself. Not yet.

#

Actually, it was not Max who raised the issue, it was Lucy. After a week of being disturbed by Max's nightmares, listening to him call out strange things in the night, she mentioned it one evening during dinner.

Lena was not there. She had woken that morning with a cold. When she had asked Agnes for a face mask, to cover her nose and mouth, protecting the rest of the family from catching the germ, she had been told that on the island they did not wear them. This was something of a surprise. On the mainland, anyone suffering from a contagious disease such as a cough or cold, wore a face mask at all times. This limited the spread of germs. It was known that the body needed to build its own resistance to such germs, so once a year, at a time that was convenient for work and family, people took 'flu days'. They would be given a regulated dose of the latest flu germ and have a week at home, wearing a mask to protect their family. Young children were often dosed at the same time, so the immunity could be conveniently built together. Parents kept records, charting the illness and dates, so everyone knew which infections they had antibodies for. This week of illness, though uncomfortable, ensured that everyone built up a healthy immune system.

Agnes explained that they did not have access to the regulated germs on the island, so the healthiest option was to catch the illness when it occurred naturally. The pharmaceutical companies would not send delivery drones to the island, believing the deliveries would be insecure. Lena was loathe to give the illness to her husband when he had so recently been in hospital, so she had quarantined herself and was remaining in her bedroom.

The family sat with John and Agnes around the scrubbed wooden table in the kitchen. It was warm and the windows had steamed up, blurring the blackness of the night beyond the panes. John said grace, thanking God for providing the food. Max wondered if it was necessary to thank God at every meal. Could they not just say one thank you that covered every meal for the whole year? They tended to say the same words anyway, it felt meaningless to him.

Agnes placed a white china pot on the table. As she lifted the lid, Max saw vegetables in a spicy sauce. More vegetables. They ate an awful lot of vegetables on the island. They did sometimes have meat but usually only once a week. There were chickens in a coop next to the pathway to the beach, and a farmer on the island raised pigs and cows. This meal was meat free though. Agnes had seasoned it with cardamom and cumin, the heavy scent rising from the pot. It was a good smell, thought Max, but it was crying out for some fried chicken to accompany it.

Den rose to take a plateful upstairs for Lena. John went to take it from him, knowing that Lena wanted to limit Den's exposure to germs but he was waved down again. Den wanted to do this, to feel useful, slightly human again. Being hospitalised had been strangely dehumanising, part of his recovery involved leaving that feeling of uselessness behind him.

He carried the tray of food to Lena. She thanked him, her nose red and sore like a beacon in her pale face. When he returned everyone was eating, hungrily chewing fresh bread and forkfuls of the casserole. He pulled up his chair and raised his own fork, then paused.

"Are we not going to say grace today?" he asked.

"We already did, Dad," said Lucy, "before you went upstairs".

Den looked momentarily confused, searching his memory for the prayer. It was not there. He shrugged. He was beginning to become used to forgetting things, comfortable that in time his brain would mend.

Lucy put down her fork and peered at Max.

"You had another one of those dreams last night," she accused. "You shouted out again. Like you were scared. It woke me up. You wake me up every night now. What's it about?"

Max chewed his food. This was unexpected. He knew that he was having lots of nightmares, knew that sometimes he woke Lucy. He hadn't expected her to blurt it out though, not in front of everyone. He glared at her.

"It's just a dream. Probably from having to sleep on the floor. Perhaps I should swap, sleep in the bed for a bit, let you have a turn on the floor."

John looked at him. "What dream?" he asked.

"It's about Midra," stated Lucy, pleased to have the attention, keen to cause Max some discomfort. Perhaps the grownups would tell him off, move him to his own room so she wouldn't have to share anymore. She felt that he had received enough acclamation for his trip to collect their father; it would be good to see him subdued a little.

John stopped eating and gave Max his full attention, this might be important. He had felt that there was more to the boy's expedition to the mainland than he had told them, sensed that he was holding something back. Perhaps he would tell them now.

Max tore a piece of crust from his bread and put it into his mouth. He chewed slowly, needing time to think. He would quite like some answers, to know what that strange room had been, to find out exactly what was happening in the hospital. He would have preferred less of an audience though. There was silence, everyone waited. John was watching him, so was his father. Lucy had returned to her meal, a smug smile curling her mouth, her eyes innocent.

Agnes stood, refilled the water jug then topped up everyone's glass. Some slopped out, formed a small puddle on the table. No one moved to wipe it up. It sat there, glistening in the lamp light. Max decided to speak.

"It was in the hospital," began Max. "I was trying to find Dad and I was worried they might catch me, that I might be in trouble. So I hid. In a trolley. And they wheeled me into a room, with a guard - a person guard not a computer - in blue clothes, like you see on the news bulletins.

"There were beds in the room, three of them. It looked like Midra in each bed. Except it wasn't him, it was his son and grandson and brother. Or some other people. But they all looked like him. It was weird." He stopped. He was not sure if he could explain why it was so disturbing, what it was that had freaked him out so badly. He remembered the bright lights, the smell of chemicals, the whir and hiss of machines, those still faces like masks. He shivered.

John spoke very quietly. He did not need to ask who Midra was, no one did. He was by far the most powerful man in the world, had led the Global Council for as long as anyone could remember. John's eyes were searching Max's, looking for answers where perhaps there were none.

"Did they see you? Did they speak?"

103

"No, no, nothing like that. They were asleep I think, or very ill. It looked like a machine was breathing for them and there were lots of tubes. Except they didn't look ill. Their faces I mean. They weren't sort of ill-looking, you know, like when you have flu or something. They just looked asleep. Not ill but asleep. But really really asleep, like they might not ever wake up."

"Why haven't you mentioned this before?" asked his father, then paused. Perhaps he had. Perhaps he had told Den all about it already, several times in fact and Den had forgotten. It was possible. He hated not being able to trust his own mind. But Max did not accuse him of forgetting, he just looked at his plate, stirred his food, seemed reluctant to speak.

"I don't know. It didn't seem important." his voice trailed off. He didn't want to say that he thought he might get into trouble. He knew there had been security around the room, had heard the checkpoints, seen the guards. He wasn't sure if he had broken any laws, if his father would feel he had a moral responsibility to report his son to the authorities. Nor did he want to admit that it had shaken him and caused him to have nightmares.

John rose from the table.

"Thank you for telling us Max," he said. "I don't expect it's important. You all finish eating; I'll be back in a minute." He nodded at Agnes and left the kitchen.

Agnes lifted the large serving spoon.

"Now, there's plenty left, who will have some more? Max, would you be very kind and pop upstairs for me, ask your mother if she would like more? Lucy, I have something in the fridge that I think you'll enjoy for pudding. Can you clear the plates while I get it?" She carried the casserole back to the hob, replaced the lid, put the spoon in the sink. Her back ached and she was tired. It was hard work catering for an extra four people. She liked the family, was fond of them even, but it was all extra. She didn't mind, knew

104

it was her duty, what she was meant to do. Sometimes she felt exhausted though. Perhaps she was growing too old for this role.

After a few minutes, John returned to the meal. He had sent the email; she would arrive before they had finished eating.

Chapter Six

Clones

The two men walked along the cliff edge. The grass was bent almost flat by the wind and it was a challenge to breathe, to draw great gulps of oxygen into their lungs, to keep the blood pumping furiously as they strode along. The sea crashed onto the beach below them, fighting with the wind to be the dominant sound. Seagulls circled, carried by the wind into great arcs before gliding to their nests in the rocks. Both men were enjoying it. Den was surprised and impressed by the pace that John had set. He wondered just how old he was, then gave up. When people reached a certain age, they were just 'old', the degree of old ceased to matter.

They walked because they wanted to talk and it helped to take the stress out of the situation, gave them both something else to look at, distract them, while they tackled some difficult ideas. And they both had things they wanted to say, issues that they needed to raise, things that would be unwelcome to the hearer.

They were walking on the opposite side of the island to where the cave entrance to the tunnel was, away from the sand dunes. If they walked far enough they would arrive at the little cove that served as a harbour to the few fishing boats that stopped occasionally. It was still windy though. Everywhere on the island was windy.

For a while they walked in silence, each deep in thought, each remembering the previous evening's conversation. Or *interrogation*, as Den thought of it. He was angry, had felt the need to defend his son though was unsure what against.

As soon as they had finished eating supper the evening before, John had ushered Max and Den back into his study. They were somewhat surprised to find another visitor waiting for them.

Nargis, the woman who Lena had seen on the beach. Max had not even noticed her that day, when she had walked towards them, her hijab flapping in the wind, keen to welcome them, make contact. Now she sat in the high backed green leather chair, very upright, very alert. She did not smile when they entered, merely nodded a greeting at John. John offered no explanation, no apology for the sudden visit. He simply closed the door firmly behind them, indicated where they should sit – Max directly opposite Nargis – then waited for her to speak.

She spoke first to Den, introducing herself, explaining that she had some medical training, had worked at the hospital and now lived on the island. As she spoke, Den had watched her. Her brown eyes were solemn beneath her hijab, her hands rested tidily on her lap and her jeans clad legs were folded neatly under her chair. Her whole body illustrated calm, self-control, strength. Here was a woman used to taking charge.

She then turned to Max, fixing him with that intense stare. When at last she spoke, she didn't bother with pleasantries.

"I hear that when you visited the hospital you went into another room? John said it had disturbed you, you found it strange. It is a shame you didn't inform us earlier, but never mind. Perhaps you will still remember enough to be of use. Please describe it to me, in as much detail as you can remember. I might be able to tell you what it was."

Max wasn't sure that he wanted to tell her. He shuffled awkwardly on his low chair, pushing his fingers into the crack between the cushions. He was not sure if he was going to be punished, if he had broken laws by being there, if by speaking he might incriminate himself. He glanced at his father for help but he was staring at Nargis, frowning, clearly suspicious.

"I'm not sure if I really remember it properly," he had begun, stopping when he saw her face, the seriousness of her expression.

107

"Max, you are not in trouble. No one on the island will punish you. No one will report you to the authorities. We just need to know about that room, to know if what we suspect is true." She was almost pleading, willing him to speak.

Max relented, influenced by her intensity. He told her about the room. She asked lots of questions, wanting details about the patients, what exactly had made Max think it was Midra? What was he wearing? Where was the room? Were there any dominant smells? Could he hear anything from other rooms? Could Max find his way there again? Was it definitely above ground-floor level? How many people had he heard? What did they say each time they checked the porter's bar code? How did Max know what they were doing? Were they all human, or could they have been bots – could Max have been hearing the simulated voices of machines? Could he describe the guard? Were they armed? Had he noticed any other security?

Max answered as fully as he could. There were so many questions. He didn't enjoy thinking about that adventure, remembering how frightened he had been, how much his legs had hurt from cramp. He thought about his fear of being incinerated, and how much he had wanted his mother, had felt like a child. He tried to keep to the facts, to answer all her questions in the hope that she would explain that strange room to him. When he finished speaking, she paused, letting the information settle, deciding how much to reveal. She then turned to Den.

"We think we know what that room is. We have suspected for a long time that Midra is receiving special medical advantages, that he has lived, healthily, for longer than is naturally possible. We suspect that what Max saw are his clones. They are physically healthy but brain dead, kept alive by machines. In effect, some would argue, not human.

"Mankind has for centuries had the technology to do this, to clone a human being, to create a person genetically identical to the donor. The advantages are huge, of course. It means that should an organ fail, cancer develop, any major disease cause damage, the donor has a spare part. The clone's body is completely compatible, parts can safely be transplanted to the donor with no fear of rejection, the body recognises it as its own. They obviously need to be age appropriate. You cannot for example, transplant a teenager's heart into an old man, his capillaries wouldn't cope with the force of the blood. Nor do you want a clone of the same age, one whose organs will be deteriorating at the same stage as the donor's. I think that is why there are several clones, of different ages, each one growing older at a steady rate.

"However, there are too many ethical problems, such as whether the clone is human or not, so it has never been certified. Even though they can produce a brain-dead clone, one incapable of independent thought, society would never sanction it. It is not allowed, not legal. It would also take up too much space, too much time, so is not economically viable. Each clone has to grow and live at the same rate as the donor, they cannot speed up the ageing process.

"We have wondered for a while though if the Global Council was using clones to keep our rulers alive, if a select few had decided to access the technology, to secretly sanction clones for themselves, to keep the Council stable. Our rulers rule for life. Unless they resign, which is rare, they are only ever replaced when they die. It has kept the world stable, no elections to hinder long term policies, no need to make populist decisions."

She turned back to Max, had thanked him for the information. Then she left, saying that they might need to return and speak to him again. John showed her out, then offered Den coffee, Max some ice cream. The discussion ended as abruptly as it had started.

No explanations, no reasons, no revealing who 'they' were. Nor what they intended to do with the information.

Today, as Den walked, he still felt uneasy. He was not sure if his son was in any danger, if the authorities would try to silence him if they knew what he had witnessed. If he was in danger of being altered himself.

And who was Nargis? He had a lot of suspicions about a Muslim, especially one who wore a hijab. He decided this was the easiest topic, the one he was mostly likely to get answers for, he would tackle it first. He stopped, facing the cliff edge. John joined him and they stood, side by side, staring across the sea as it rushed towards the land, determined to force itself as far onto the sand as it could, each wave chasing the next, never ending, never losing energy, never stopping to consider if the action was logical. Not unlike humanity.

"Tell me about Nargis," he began, "Tell me why a Muslim is on the island. Especially one who wears a hijab. I don't remember the last time I saw one being worn, such a militant statement of defiance."

John stooped, picked up a rock, hurled it forwards. They watched it as it curled downwards, dropping into the edge of the water. Den nodded appreciatively. Good throw.

"Let me start at the beginning, give you the long version," said John. "It might save some time in the end, be less confusing. Is that okay? It will be a lot of listening."

Den nodded. He still found it difficult to concentrate, and his short term memory was worse than unreliable. But it was improving. A week on the island, without constant stress, had been good for him. He was feeling less fuzzy, more in control.

John spoke slowly, choosing his words with care, wanting the other man to understand.

"The Global Council has, over the years, done a lot of good things for humanity. Many of the decisions, the new laws, are sensible. They have stopped humanity destroying the planet and destroying themselves. We think this is good. They have policies to combat poverty, have made the world a fairer place to live; there are no starving children or populations with inadequate medical care. There are no wars, no terrorist threats. The climate has stopped changing for the worse, animals have stopped becoming extinct. There has been greater funding for technological progress and medical research. I applaud these things, we would be lost without them. The world acting as a single unit, populations all working together, seems to have solved many of the age-old problems that threatened to swamp us.

"However, we also think they have overstepped their brief, touched on matters which they should have left alone. The main one, of course, is religion. When man tries to be equal to God, or decides he does not need God, things go wrong, become out of sync, off-kilter. It is not how we were intended to live. Man is physical, mental AND spiritual. We should never make the mistake of denying that.

"On the island, we try to help those people who refuse to live like that, those who believe that there is one God. And that He is God, not some religious equivalent who can be kept in a box, got out and worshipped when convenient, prayed to in times of trouble and then put away, forgotten until the next time. God is God, whether people choose to recognise Him or not. The Global Council cannot change that, whatever they do."

"But Nargis is a Muslim," persisted Den. "She doesn't believe in the same God that we do. Hers is a different religion."

"A different religion, yes," agreed John. "But God is not confined to a religion. As I said, God is God. People can choose to

111

believe about Him what they will, it will not change His God-ness."

"Yes," said Den, "I know that. But you are implying that we all wander around in ignorance, that God has not revealed Himself at all. I cannot accept that.

"I do believe in God. I also believe He has taught us about Himself in the Bible. He taught us about *why* He created us, that we are special to Him. The Bible explains that we kept doing things wrong; we moved away from Him, that He became a man, took human form as Jesus and died. So that we can be forgiven. I believe all that." Den paused, searching for the right words. The wind was rushing against his face and he was almost shouting in an effort to be heard. "And I believe that Jesus didn't stay dead, that he came back to life. The Bible tells us that now God will forgive us if we ask, that we can know Him, have a relationship with Him, a friendship. He will listen to us, talk to us, help us.

"It also tells us that Jesus will come back again. That in the last times, at the end of the world, Jesus will come. That everyone who believes in him will be saved, taken to God, where we belong, where we have a place, a home." He swallowed, feeling he had given a fair description of what he believed the Christian faith to be about. Now to tackle Islam.

He continued, "This is not what Muslims believe. I do not believe that '*all religions lead to God*'. If I did, I wouldn't be here, wouldn't be a threat to the Council. If I believed that, I would have been content in those awful holy places, worshipping my little god and letting everyone else worship theirs. There would be no definite right and wrong. No, I'm sorry, I cannot compromise on this one. Everyone has the right to believe what they want, but that does *not* make everything right. And if what I believe is right, what Muslims believe must be wrong. Sorry, that's just how it is."

112

Den paused. The words had come in a rush, full of passion. Almost like something he had learnt by rote. His brain felt suddenly tired. Maybe he was not ready for this conversation. The wind was causing his head to ache and he was so tired that he felt slightly dizzy. He was finding this now - he would seem completely well, back to his old strength, but after a quick burst of intelligent conversation or listening to music, he would feel exhausted.

But he wanted to know. He needed to know, what was going on, what the purpose of the island was, if there was a plan. He needed to know if his family were safe. And it all seemed to be tied up with faith, with what he believed and with the Global Council. He needed to know. He settled back and prepared to listen.

Counting Stars

The men stood at the cliff edge, looking out to sea. There was a boulder nearby, covered in lichen but clean. They moved towards it, rested against it. Den used his arms to haul himself onto it, sat there, like a child playing '*king of the castle*'. He could feel its damp coldness seeping through his trousers, but it was not uncomfortable. It helped to steady him. The wind ruffled his hair, tugging at the roots where it was newly grown after having it shaved in the hospital. It was cold, and he wished he had thought to wear a hat. He listened to the waves crashing, waiting for John to speak, to explain.

"I believe in the same Bible that you do," said John, wanting to find common ground, for the other man to listen, to not leap ahead with narrow views that he had accepted but perhaps never challenged. He knew that he needed his help, wanted to make it as easy as possible. He was an intelligent man, so John felt he could be honest. He picked a fat blade of grass, began to smooth it in his fingers as he spoke.

"In Genesis, right at the beginning, we learn about why things are as they are. About man's early relationship with God. It is also where we first meet Abraham. God made a promise to him, that he would have many offspring. He took Abraham outside, showed him the stars in the sky and told him to count them. He said his offspring would be even more than the stars."

Den nodded impatiently. Yes, he knew this. He thought it irrelevant to the conversation.

"Yes, but that promise passed through Isaac, who was a Jew. Later Jesus was born as a Jew. Then Christianity grew up, following the teaching of Jesus. I am a Christian. Not a Jew. Certainly not a Muslim."

"And yet," smiled John, "perhaps you are a star. Perhaps that promise passed downwards to include those *spiritual* 'children' of Abraham. Perhaps it included Christians?"

Den gave a curt bow. He had heard this before, knew that people felt the promise to Abraham applied to Christians after Jesus had come. He felt they were straying from the point rather. What about Nargis? She was clearly not a Christian. Not even a Jew.

"I am not sure you are correct about Muslims," said John. "If you read a bit more, after Abraham's concubine Hagar had run away with his son Ishmael, didn't God also come to her? Didn't He repeat the promise? Say that He would make Ishmael into a great nation? Which He did of course, Ishmael is thought to be the beginning of the Arab race. Who are Muslim... Could it be that they are stars too?"

Den frowned, this did not sound correct, didn't fit with his theology. They were a completely different religion, had different beliefs. He felt John was twisting things, using clever arguments to make something illogical sound plausible.

John waited. There was no hurry. These were big ideas, they needed time to settle, be considered. He lifted the blade of grass, stretched it between his thumbs and forefingers, used it as a reed, blew. The sound was loud, even in the wind. Den smiled.

"But," argued Den returning to the discussion, "Muslims have different beliefs to us. They think we are wrong, the enemy."

"Did Jews accept Christianity?" asked John, "Did they happily embrace the new religion when Jesus came? I don't think so! They were furious. They rejected Jesus, to the point of killing him. But are they still stars? Are they still a special race to God? I think so. I think it is for God to decide what will happen, not us. We should let God be God."

"What about when Jesus comes again?" said Den. "The Muslims believe that everyone who is a true Muslim will be called to God, everyone else, especially the Christians, will be destroyed."

"Yes," agreed John, "some Muslims do believe that. However, does what man believes alter the will of God? If we get things wrong does He change his actions?

"Think about when Jesus came the first time. He was promised to the Jewish race. They knew this. Did they know he would come as a baby? Did they know he would teach them about God? That he would challenge their religious practices?

"No! They thought he would come as a mighty warrior, that he would save them from their enemies. Even when Jesus was with them, living beside them, teaching them, many people thought he would lead a revolt against the occupying Roman Empire. So did their misconceptions change anything? Did it mean they were no longer stars? No longer God's chosen people? Did God change the plan? Of course not. God is God. Who is man to challenge Him? Jesus still came to the Jews. Some accepted him, some did not. But their wrong expectations did not change God's plan.

115

"Go back even further, all the way to Abraham. Did he get it right? Did he understand what God was telling him? God *told* him that he would have a son to be his heir. Did Abraham fully understand? Did he know that his wife Sarah would bear him a son? No, he translated God's message in his own way, he had a son through Sarah's servant. So did that stop God? Did He change His plan to fit in with Abraham's misunderstanding? No. God is God. He does not change His mind."

He paused, watching a gull as it swooped towards the sea, then seemed to float upwards, seemingly weightless as it charted the air currents, used them to glide. It appeared very small, so was a distance from them. Its creamy feathers contrasting with the dark sky as storm clouds began to gather. The sun was very bright, almost falsely so, as if pretending that the rain would not begin to fall, the sky would not darken to an almost twilight gloom. The weather held its breath in anticipation, waiting for the storm which was about to break.

John explained, "Personally, I think the Muslims are wrong. I think that God is not limited to the Muslim religion, just as He is not limited to the Jewish religion. Just as, dare I say it, He is not limited to the Christian religion. God is bigger than any religion. He has chosen to reveal Himself to us, but we must never presume to know God completely, to be equal with Him. We only see a little part, what He chooses to reveal to us. Some things are for God, not us. We must just do what we believe is right. For me, on this island, I believe I should be helping people like you, people who I believe are those long-ago-promised 'stars'.

"I also do *not* think 'all religions lead to God'. I have never said that. However, I do think that sometimes we try to limit God, to make Him fit our own image of Him. He has revealed Himself to us but sometimes we add our own views to those truths, we think He has said things which actually He has not. We do like our

116

religions. God has never really been about religion. God is God; we are simply invited to worship Him, to let Him be our God. Sometimes it is helpful to go back, to read what was actually written, to remember that God does not change, is not fickle like people. God said those stars were special. Who am I to disagree, just because some are not saying the things I think they should?"

He spread out his arm towards the sea.

"Look at those waves," he said.

Den looked. They were ferocious, chasing each other onto the land as if they would break it. Great rolling masses of water, churning with power, unleashed energy.

"Below those waves," said John, "are plants, seaweed. They are thrown about in the currents, rootless. I think that people who deny God are like that. They cannot resist the ebb and tide of the times, they are at the mercy of waves.

"Now look at that tree," he instructed.

Den looked. The tree was bowed, straining in the wind, its branches stretched forth like arms, its trunk leaning.

"We are to be like a tree," said John. "We must have roots that are very strong, firmly placed in what is true. But if we are rigid, if we are not prepared to bend as that tree is bending, then we will snap. We must have roots, we must be sure of our faith. We must not be rigid, we must not be held by our religion. There is a difference. Soon it will be very important that people are sure where they stand".

"Do you think these are the '*End Times*' then?" asked Den. "That Jesus is about to come again, the world is about to end?" A fat drop of water landed on the rock next to him. Then another. They did not have long.

"I cannot presume to know that," said John. "I do know that while we in the West were comfortable, had freedom of religion, we lost the urgency of thinking about the last times. Now we are not so complacent, we feel it is very close. However, in some parts of the world, like Asia, people have suffered for their faith for centuries. They have been very aware of the hardship they suffer for what they believe, they have been much better at looking to God than perhaps we have. It is why we send people to Asia. The stars there are better practiced at living life under oppression, they have much to teach us. Their governments are now less radical, they voted for leaders who would not enforce the Global Council's laws quite so rigorously.

"But now we must discuss the Global Council and the things that Max told us."

He paused, looked again across the ocean, breathed in its vastness. It made him feel small and he liked that, thought it healthy for man to realise how tiny he was in the universe. It was beginning to rain properly now. He beckoned to Den, began to retrace their steps. He continued to speak as they walked.

"I told you that we try to help the people who we consider to be 'stars'. That is only partly the truth. We also want to change things here, to improve how things are done," he called, raising his voice so he could be heard as they quickened their pace, keen to not be soaked.

"Now, the Global Council has been stable for many many years. People have begun to comment about the age of the rulers. As I said, we suspected that some may be using clones but until now, we have never been able to prove that, have not had any evidence. I think that what Max told us changes things. Perhaps. It is not proof, but it is evidence.

"Of all the people on the Global Council, the one most emphatically against belief in a single God is Midra. It is almost as if he takes it personally that he might not be the most powerful being that exists. He has instigated all of the religious laws, he now stringently upholds them. It is unfortunate for us that he is not only

118

on the *Global* Council but also happens to live in England, so also decides how our country will interpret the laws set by the Council.

"We think that if we can remove him, then we can introduce a new ruler. One who would be more tolerant. Who would allow freedom of belief. The other rulers would be unlikely to question it. We know that some are unhappy with the law as it stands, they feel it has served its purpose, removed the threat of terrorism, it is now unnecessary.

"Come, we need to hurry, this storm is moving in. We can discuss this in more detail another time."

The two men began to trot, the rain falling now in fat droplets, each one very wet. Neither wore a coat, it wasn't cold. The wind was behind them and the homeward journey went quickly.

As they walked, Den considered what he had been told. He was not sure what he thought about the religious part, about them all being those 'stars', too many to be counted. But he knew what he thought about interfering with the government. He was not sure exactly what they were thinking of but he knew it could have dire consequences. He did not like it. He did not like it at all.

Chapter Seven

The Cave Conference

They did not continue their discussion for several days. Den used the time to reconnect with his family a little, to spend time with Lena, to walk with Max and build sand empires with Lucy. His brain was gradually becoming less fuzzy. He still often forgot things but his tendency to repeat whole conversations just minutes after having them was reducing. He would have said that he never repeated himself at all now, though he couldn't be sure. He did sometimes start to do something – to turn off a lamp, to recharge his computer, to return a dirty cup to the kitchen – only to find it had already been done, *he* had already done it but forgotten. Little things that were unimportant but annoying. Incidents that made him realise that he still couldn't trust his brain. Not quite, not yet.

When they did finally speak again about the clones, they were joined by Lena, Agnes and Nargis. It was still light, the last of the day seeping away, the sky the colour of dirty washing up water. The children were in bed, Max playing computer games, Lucy supposedly sleeping. They were again outside, this time walking towards the cave. When Den asked why there were outside, John explained that they were less likely to be overheard. True, there were drones, tiny microphones that could hover overhead. But if one was looking, they could be seen. It was not possible to manufacture an invisible one. However, if they talked inside, the authorities could pinpoint any point of the building with a laser, which could use vibrations to detect sound. Technicians could transfer these back to voices. Den was still not sure who 'they' were but he understood that no conversation held inside a building should be considered completely private. This was somewhat unnerving.

They did not speak much as they walked, simply followed in a line towards the cave. Lena and Nargis chatted about inconsequential things, the children, what the weather would do. As they walked Lena glanced at Nargis's hijab. It kept her hair neatly hidden, the wind tugging at the corners of the cloth but leaving her unruffled. In comparison, Lena felt large and crumpled. She was much taller than the other woman and her hair was a mobile mess, carried in all directions by the wind, and frequently in her eyes and mouth. She wished she had thought to tie it back.

Nargis saw the other woman looking at her and her mouth curled.

"Agnes told me that you feel my hijab is too militant, an aggressive display of my religion," she said. "It's ironic really because the opposite is true. Islam is a very modest religion; I cover my head to show my modesty, not to flaunt my beliefs."

Lena was unsure how to respond. She felt herself colour, was embarrassed, made a mental note not to be too open with Agnes in the future.

Agnes, walking behind the other women, was tired. She was here because she needed to be, but she would have preferred to stay at home, to have a nap, maybe tidy up a little. Lena tried to help with the cooking but she was not very practical, tending to cause more work than she got done. The burnt vegetables and lumpy sauces were a waste of food and Agnes was having a hard time biting her tongue, saying nothing, determined to run a peaceful household. Now, her wrinkled face was expressionless, eyes blank, following the group and wondering what her husband would say. She knew he had a plan, had already made decisions. Her role was to support.

She was at least sleeping better now. Den had taken John to one side, said he was worried about her, suggested that he and Lena vacate their bedroom and move to another cottage. The nearest cottage had space, and the inhabitants were willing to share the space. That was how the island worked, a small community with a common goal, bound together by tension and necessity.

They arrived at the entrance to the cave and found three people waiting for them, two men and a woman. The three did not introduce themselves, simply said hello to Lena and Den, soundlessly hugged John and Agnes and suggested they move to the drier ground within the cave. Lena watched, felt as though she was on the edge of something, an observer of close friends but not part of the group. Nargis held up her computer, scanned the sky, nodded to let them know that the sky was clear, no drones detected.

They walked into the gloomy interior of the cave, smelling the dry salt smell of seaweed. Agnes spread blankets, pulled from John's backpack, onto the rock surface and they sat. It was hard but clean. The cold crept through the twisted wool, seeping into her bones, pressing hard into the base of her back. She hoped this would not take too long and moved to the edge of the group, where she could lean against a shelf of rock. It was cruelly hard but at least it offered some support.

One of the men went outside, to stand watch, give the alert if a listening drone was spotted.

Nargis opened the conversation. She said that she had informed the others and they were all in agreement - now was the time to act. Den wondered who 'the others' were, decided not to ask. Yet.

John cleared his throat and took the lead in the discussion. He knew what they needed to achieve, had clear goals and intended to manipulate the group into acting as he wanted. He was good at that. When he was younger, still at work, his staff had named him 'The Puppeteer'. He was not sure they had meant it as a compliment but he had acknowledged that it was accurate. He generally managed to make things happen. He was not afraid of making decisions on behalf of others, wise ones of course, ones that benefited the greater good. So often people made wrong choices, it was important to provide direction.

He began by stating what they all knew, that the current political climate was unfairly targeting religion and needed to change. The main instigator and enforcer of the religious laws was Midra. If he died and was replaced, then it was likely that the current laws would be relaxed.

Nargis frowned.

"Are you suggesting we harm him directly? I do not think I could sanction that."

John noted her clouded eyes, the worry crinkling her brown forehead, knew that she was thinking of her children, fearful of how an openly criminal act might affect them if she were involved. He shook his head, raised a tanned, gnarled hand in denial. She would be unpersuadable on this; it was not worth trying to change her mind.

"No, no, I do not believe that will be necessary. As you know, we believe that he has stayed alive artificially, using clones to replace body parts that may have become infected or deteriorated to an unhealthy degree. He is very old. We believe that if we can destroy the clones, infect them in some way, remove his ability to regenerate, then he will naturally die very soon."

Nargis nodded. She was silent, thinking for a moment, considering scenarios. She agreed that now was the time to stop Midra in his quest for eternal life. She felt that, even if they had opportunity, killing him would be wrong, not in keeping with the beliefs they were all trying to protect. However, 'removing' his clones, upsetting what was little more than an experiment, was acceptable. If they could remove his access to constant transplants, a healthy supply of blood transfusions, fresh organs, then his life would naturally end very soon. One could not live forever and he had already used up more than his natural number of years. When she spoke it was with quiet confidence.

"I can source something that would be effective. Something that could be injected. It would be better than just destroying their life-support machines, would delay the destruction a bit, give whoever does it longer to escape. I can get something that would cause damage within a few hours, a day perhaps before anything was noticed. By which time the damage would be irreversible, they would have no choice but to destroy the clones.

"Our problem would be how to collect it. It would be suspicious for any of us to return to the mainland and I wouldn't want to trust any of our normal delivery routes."

"Couldn't someone just walk through the tunnel to collect it?" asked Lena. She knew the other woman, the one sitting stiffly to her left, had walked through the tunnel for the meeting. She looked at her, noticed her tightly bound hair, her erect back and high collared shirt. Not a fashionable young woman. She had not yet spoken, and Lena had no impression of her other than her formal exterior. Everything about her looked tense, almost cross.

"Not really," said Nargis. "The main problem would be where to collect it. People do not collect medical supplies from the pharmacies directly, as you know, they are always couriered to the patient's home. I could arrange for my contact to package the goods but they would need to be collected from an address on the mainland. The problem would arise afterwards, when the clones had been destroyed. The authorities would trace the source of the chemical used, and follow the trail to the address where it was delivered. It would mean we would lose another of our mainland contacts, as they would have to flee their home as soon as the clones were destroyed.

"We could collect it ourselves, from our own address on the mainland, as we have left anyway. But it would be naive to think one of us could go back unobserved, and we do not have a valid reason to do so. The tunnels are only used in emergency situations, or important ones, like this meeting." She nodded at the woman next to Lena, who had made the journey today because it had been deemed essential for her to be there and electronic communication was too open. Nargis continued, "We are watched, you see. While we remain on the island, the authorities are happy to more or less ignore us. But an unexplained trip to the mainland would raise interest. Interest that might lead to investigative work in the hospital".

At the mention of hospital, Den shivered, feeling suddenly queasy. Too many memories rushed back, flooding his mind with bright lights, injections, lack of control, pain and confusion. He took a breath, hoped no one noticed.

John noted his change of pallor but said nothing. Lena did not notice, she was stung by Nargis's words, wondering if she was being referred to as 'naive'. She turned away, examined the wall beside her for a while, not trusting herself to speak. The rock was discoloured, covered in green and the remains of barnacle shells, dried out long ago when the tides ceased to penetrate this far into the cave. She reached out a hand, touched the sharp edges of a broken shell, pretended she was barely listening. She felt excluded from this group, though could not quite understand why.

"I'm not sure why the family is staying on the island," said one of the men. "Surely we've learnt everything now that the boy can tell us? Isn't it safer for them to leave? There's no reason for them to stay, the authorities will be wondering why they haven't moved on. Won't it just raise suspicions, them being here?"

Lena was not sure she liked her family being discussed as though they were not present, had no say in what happened to them. She opened her mouth to speak, then closed it again. May be wiser to just listen for a while. The feeling of sitting outside an inner ring, of not being a part of the group was even stronger now. It made her feel like an adolescent again, excluded from a friendship group while they whispered in front of her.

John shook his head. "No, for now they should stay. We might need the boy to help us gain access." He wanted Den to stay for longer, knew the parents would never leave without the children, considered the risks were outweighed by the potential advantages. This thing, this mission, was bigger than one family. It was bigger than all of them.

Lena was about to protest, was fairly bursting at the description of Max as 'the boy', when she was interrupted by the woman to her left.

"Well, whatever you decide, it needs to be quick," she said. "Our research with 3-D printing of human organs is almost complete. I estimate that within five months, organ replacement using genetically exact replicas that have been printed using donor tissue will be viable and in the public domain. It took us much longer to complete than we thought, but we're nearly there now. That means life expectancy will rocket to new lengths. If we want to encourage change within the Global Council, we need to get a move on."

She stopped speaking as abruptly as she had started.

Everyone looked at her but she had said her piece, had nothing more to say. She was here to impart information, not to help them make plans. She would leave that to those whose minds had room for creativity, her own was fully occupied with science and absolutes. If the plan they decided upon needed her help, she would give it. As long as it did not compromise her position on the mainland, of course. She held a senior position at work, could help the group better if her cover remained intact. Even coming here today had been a risk, she was not convinced that John had been right to insist. She wondered how much longer they needed to sit in this cold cave, when she could return to the comforting cleanliness of her laboratory.

Turning to Nargis, she asked in a low voice what she intended to use to damage the clones. Hearing the chemical name, she said nothing, merely raising her eyebrows, impressed that the other woman could access such a thing.

"Do you think the Council will sanction it?" asked John. He had known that 3-D printers were being used to copy human tissue, that there were experiments with 3-D bio-printing in the hope they could copy viable organs. However, even if they achieved it, would its use be sanctioned? It would enable people to live for much longer, would create a sudden blip in all human life expectancy. The population size at the moment was tightly controlled, the Council hoped to bring it down to sustainable levels so that the planet would not be overcrowded, under-resourced, over-polluted. He was not sure that they would allow a sudden, artificially induced, extension to life expectancy, with the knock-on effect of increased population levels. Not for the general public anyway.

The woman nodded, understanding his thoughts.

"I think if it was made public, it would be hard to contain its use. But even if they did stop it leaking, somehow kept people from talking, I doubt they would resist the opportunity themselves. I foresee a Global Council who are almost constant, who all outlive those whom they are governing. So it's important we get someone in place who will govern well."

Lena and Den saw the others nod in agreement, something unspoken in their eyes. It was clear they were all thinking the same thoughts, had someone in mind who was ready and willing to join the Council. Someone who would be chosen. Someone who would govern in the style that would suit this group. Someone less oppressive than Midra.

127

Ideas and Memories

It was at the mention of 3-D printers that a plan began to form in Lena's mind. It was Lucy's birthday soon and she had wanted to buy her something special, to compensate slightly for having hauled her away from her friends and home. She had wondered about giving her a replica doll but had been unsure if it was possible to get one on the island. Replica dolls were all the fashion at the moment. Several companies manufactured them.

The idea was a simple one. You sent photographs of a certain specification to the manufacturers and they produced a tiny lifelike replica of the child. They used 3-D printers and the results were startling. She knew that Den found them slightly creepy, thinking it would be strange to have a plastic copy of your own child; but girls of Lucy's age loved them. It was possible to buy identical clothes for the doll and the child, so dressing up games could be combined with having a doll, something to care for. It was possible to get boy replica dolls but Max had never wanted one, being more action based with his activities and less imaginative. Lucy however, would adore one. Lena had had it in mind for a few days now, intending to ask Agnes if it would be possible to arrange for one to be made from the island. She edged closer to the group and cleared her throat. When she spoke, her voice sounded hollow, as though the cave was absorbing it.

"I think I have an idea of why we might collect a package from home," she said. She turned to Nargis. "Could your injections be couriered to our house on the mainland?"

Nargis nodded. They would be sent by delivery drone, not person, but the meaning was the same. Neither would cross to the island, both would deliver to an address on the mainland.

Lena then shared her plan, how she wanted to buy a replica doll for Lucy, how collecting a special gift would be a perfectly legitimate reason for returning to their home, that she could collect the syringes at the same time, bring them to the island, give them to whoever was going to get them into hospital.

John leaned forwards, pleased with the idea. Den put an encouraging hand on her back. It was warm, conveyed he was proud of her, it was a good plan. Lena began to feel more accepted by this strange group, of more use.

"Yes, that might work," agreed John, "though we need to think through a few details. I agree with Michael, your continued presence on the island will soon become suspicious. Perhaps we could pretend one of the children is too ill to travel? That you are all staying until they recover?"

Nargis thought this an excellent idea, she could tell Lena some symptoms for a childhood illness, something that would require rest and medication but not be considered too serious. Lena could discuss it loudly with Lucy in the hope that someone was listening, that the authorities on the mainland would record the conversation, believe that Lucy was ill. They could then order some legitimate medicine from the hospital pharmacy, her source could add the destructive vials to the same package. It could all be delivered to the home address, collected by a parent. It was a good cover.

"I'm not sure that we need to transport the vials to the island though," said John, "it would be much better if they were taken straight to the hospital and administered on the same trip. Nargis, have you made contact yet with anyone who knows where that room is? Or better still, has access? No? Shame. Then one of us must do it. We know roughly where the clones are kept. There is a section of the hospital that is never used for the public. It seems to be almost sealed off. The staffing rosters are also interesting, with very few people working there. Even the bots, responsible for cleaning and transporting things, seem to be limited to a select few. It seems an obvious place to suspect something untoward is in progress.

"However, access and exit routes will be difficult, especially if we have no one on the inside who can legitimately enter that area. Could the watchers get us some building plans? Maybe send me the map of heating ducts and the pathways for the electrical cables? They might present an option. By person, of course, we cannot be seen to be emailing such information. It is important that we are careful."

He looked around the group, pleased with the outcome of their meeting. He stretched.

"I think that is all for now. We can meet again when we have a few things in place. I would suggest that online discussions would be unwise, we should assume all our email conversations are monitored."

The group stood, glad to leave the hard floor and damp atmosphere, to return to fresh air and daylight. Den had said nothing. He was keen to help, could see the importance of the plan. But he was worried by the involvement of his family, resolved to discuss this privately with John. He would prefer for Lena and the children to have left the island when all this went down, could see no reason for them to stay. He believed the action was necessary but was not sure if he was willing to risk harm to his family in order for it to be accomplished. John was very decided, had the gleam of the crusader in his eye. Den wondered if he was as big a threat to the welfare of his family as the Global Council, wondered if there were limits to what the other man might be willing to sacrifice for what he considered to be the greater good. Would his *'counting of stars'* be prepared to sacrifice one or two along the way?

As the group left the cave, Lena and Den walked together, behind John and Agnes. Nargis walked ahead with the two men, the other woman had bid them goodbye and disappeared deeper into the cave, towards the tunnel.

130

Lena put out her hand, grasped her husband's and for a while they walked in silence, mulling over the conversation. Lena was worried. She knew this was just the sort of adventure that excited Den, that he would see it as a 'mission', something worth taking risks for. She was more pragmatic. The family was safely off the mainland, why not just continue with their journey, escape to somewhere safer?

In direct conflict with this, she was also concerned about the conversation that Den had relayed to her about the *stars*, Abraham's descendants. She had a nagging doubt that maybe she might not qualify. She definitely believed in God, in a being higher than man, a living entity that controlled the world. But she also definitely believed it with a lot less passion than Den did. She was not as confident as he was that she ever heard God directly, her belief was more vague, a bit wishful rather than certain. She worried that this might exclude her from 'star' status. An idea was forming in her mind that maybe, if she played a role in this latest plan, if she, for example, was the one who returned to collect the medication, then maybe, just maybe, that would count towards her 'star status'. Perhaps she would have done enough to be counted as one of the chosen, she would be on the same side as her husband.

It would also mean that she could continue with her hope for a replica doll. Although that had now become unnecessary, due to the plan to pretend Lucy was ill enough to require medication, Lena still wanted to get her daughter one. She felt that Lucy deserved a treat, some compensation for having been taken from her home and friends. Lena didn't expect the others to understand, it sounded a flippant desire when compared with the seriousness of sabotaging the Global Council, didn't even begin to compare. However, for Lena, the mother and carer, it was every bit as important. If she volunteered to collect the medicine and vials, she could bring back a doll at the same time. It wouldn't hinder the 'important' plan at all, would simply be an added bonus for her. She decided to not mention it to Den, was unsure if he would agree.

She thought about the group that had just met, the motley gathering where John had very much been the leader. She wondered again about Nargis, the Muslim, could she really be the same as them, on the same side?

As if reading her thoughts, Den squeezed her hand. "You seemed to be getting along with Nargis okay. What did you talk about?"

"Nothing really. Children, cooking, weather. And her hijab. Agnes had told her it worried me. That was an embarrassing moment!

"Den, do you think they're right, John and Agnes? Do you really think that Muslims and Christians are the same? It feels wrong to me, there're too many differences."

Den thought before he answered, listening to the crunch of their feet as they crossed the shingle, holding Lena's hand tighter on the uneven ground. He still wasn't sure, though had been thinking of little else recently.

"I don't know. Certainly they hold different beliefs. I'm just not sure how much difference actually matters. I mean, look at the Catholics. We believe a lot of things that are different to them but would we actually say they were on a different side, believed in a different God? I don't think so, nor would most Catholics deny that someone of the Anglican faith had the same basic beliefs."

"But that's not the same!" protested Lena, "They haven't done the terrible things that the Muslims have done! The Muslims are the ones whose terrorist behaviour caused the Global Council to make the religious laws in the first place!"

"Actually, that's not true," Den said. He remembered.

He remembered the bombings done by the Irish Catholics, a London living in fear, the violence suffered in the name of religion.

He remembered the Spanish Inquisition, living in England and being told of the culling of anyone named as a heretic. The torture, the cruelty, all in the name of religion.

He remembered the burnings in London, the stench of human flesh under the reign of Queen Mary, the atrocities sanctioned in the name of the Pope. He remembered being a boy, running errands, when he first saw a burning. He had been drawn to the watching crowds with a horrid fascination, had heard the accusations read aloud to the convicted prisoners tied to the posts, heard them refuse to recant. Then they had lit those stacks of wood beneath them. People had jeered or wept as the flames grew higher and Den (but not Den) had left, running across cobbled streets towards home, the images seared into his eyes and mind like a brand. Never forgotten. Passed down through the generations to Den.

He remembered more burnings. In America this time, the flames souring towards the sky in a mass of blue smoke, fuelled by petrol. It was a cross burning this time. It was meant to represent Jesus, the light of the world. A large cross that had been carried by men wearing white pointed hats, their eyes black holes of smug self-righteousness, another crowd standing near, watching, doing nothing to help. There had been more weeping, the mother crying over her dead teenager, his poor body showing the marks of hatred and violence. All done in the name of Christianity. A warped Christianity that was distorted beyond recognition from the teachings of Christ.

Few people today would say these acts of violence defined what it meant to be either Catholic or Protestant. They were far removed from the basic elements of faith held by the church. As far removed as the slaughtering carried out by the Crusaders in the middle ages or the laws established by Henry the Eighth. Was it therefore fair to tarnish the whole of Islam with the actions of a few?

It was also becoming increasingly hard for him to argue against their core beliefs. It was true, they held some beliefs which he could never accept. But so too did Catholics. He could never accept that a Papal decree was equal to the Bible in authority, nor would he ever pray to saints or accept that physical items, be they relics or places, could hold spiritual significance. To his mind, that was tantamount to superstition. And yet, and yet – there was that nagging doubt. Catholics held the same basic beliefs that he did. They believed in one God, that Jesus was somehow both God and human, that humans could be forgiven. Could he deny that they were as much part of God's family as he was?

The same was true of the Jews. Most of their religion rejected the vital elements of his own. Yet, his religion was built on theirs. Could he really claim that he worshipped a different God? Could God accept them as part of his chosen race, the original 'stars' even though they had rejected Jesus? Was John right, did God remain unchanged in His plans despite people's unbelief?

So where did that leave Islam? They believed in one God, how much did it matter that they called him by a different name? And no, they did not believe that Jesus was somehow also God. But could the *actions* of Jesus, the taking of human form, the dying, the rising from the dead, be the important bit? Could it be that those actions enabled forgiveness from God, even for those who did not fully accept the historical fact of the events? Were the teachings of Mohammed, and he only knew a few of them, could it be that they did not actually contradict what the Bible taught about God? He didn't know, his knowledge of Islam was too hazy. But nor was he quite so sure that John was wrong. Not yet. Not until he had done some research on Islam.

He sighed and rubbed his head. His brain was tired. Too much thinking.

"Let's talk another time," he said.

Lena stiffened but nodded. He could tell she was annoyed, felt he was opting out of the discussion unnecessarily. They rarely had time alone, time to really talk. The cottage they were sharing was comfortable but not private. They often overheard the owners talking through the thin walls. It was more than a little inhibiting. He knew that Lena wanted to talk now, to have a proper discussion. But he was just too tired.

He found this happened frequently now. Physically, he was almost up to full strength. He could walk for miles, help John to chop wood, tend the garden, repair buildings. But anything mentally tiring, reading, intense conversations, thinking, left him feeling drained. It was hard for his family to appreciate. He looked normal. Even his hair had pretty much grown back to its original length. Most of his activities were the same as before he went to hospital. So it was difficult for them to remember that he was different. He had been altered. His ability to think, his control of emotions, his short term memory, had all changed. If he had broken his leg awkwardly, now walked with a limp or used a stick, no one would ask him to run a marathon or climb a mountain. But his own injuries were hidden, people couldn't see any visual sign of weakness. He sometimes wished he could wear a head bandage, an obvious symbol for how he felt inside. Not possible. Instead, he pulled Lena closer, gave her a hard kiss on her unruly hair and started to walk faster, pulling her towards the cottage.

Chapter Eight

Maps and Plans

The plans of the hospital arrived a week later. John was examining them in his study when Lena knocked at his door. She had wanted to use his computer, to check the finished train routes, to plan for her family to leave the island. An idea was beginning to form in her mind. She would arrange for Den and the children to leave, she would stay and help John – she felt she owed this strange island group that much, plus she hoped that doing something so supportive, something that held some risk, would add to her *star* status. She was still terribly worried that when it came to counting stars, her name would not be on the list. She desperately wanted to be on the same side as her family.

She now wanted to view the tube trains. The train routes were being completed all the time. This involved a massive building project, a great use of unskilled labour, of which there was a seemingly unending supply. When the Global Council was first introduced, it had been felt that if the world was to act as a single entity, to be global in decisions that affected disease, pollution, global warming, then it should be more unified in every way. Subsistence farming in poorer countries should be replaced with less precarious employment. Education, health care, all became standardised; nations became unified, more equal. The Global Council introduced laws and policies that covered every country. Each country had its own enforcers, who oversaw how the laws would be implemented. These individual country governments could not change laws - they were all set by the Global Council; but they did decide what actually happened in practice.

Travel between countries was encouraged. People could live and work wherever they wanted, subject to permission from the residency overseer of the country in question. This allowed for a mobile workforce, people could follow the jobs they were allocated. The Global Council invested money in creating jobs, mainly for unskilled labour, the ancient idea of being paid an allowance while being unemployed had disappeared many years ago. She and Den had both chosen their jobs, been lucky enough to find vacancies that suited them. Had this been impossible, they would have been allocated work. Everyone worked. It was considered healthy for both the individual and the population as a whole.

Passports had become redundant when bar codes were introduced. It was easy to track an individual should this be deemed necessary, as all bar codes were run from the same central computers. Every public place had scanners at the doors. Tracking movement was automatic.

Everyone belonged to the human race, they knew which ethnicity they originated from, but cultural differences were less important. Of course, festivals and traditions were an intrinsic part of life, had for most people replaced religion almost completely. Everyone celebrated those festivals that were important to them, either due to their own ethnicity or an adopted one. They were social times, an excuse for a themed party, traditional food, often gifts. They were not limited to geographic countries.

Countries that tended to be inhospitable, those that often flooded or which had frequent violent earthquakes or volcanoes, were mostly used as tourist resorts; few people lived there all year round. The first mass migration of populations had been due to historical wars. When they became unnecessary, people still naturally preferred to live in certain places and others became less populated. The solar generators were in deserts, their upkeep dependent on relatively few workers. The deserts were also a popular holiday destination, somewhere to relax for a few days, beautiful hotels with regulated temperatures and reliable water supplies. This was being made easier through the building of the railways. It was on Lena's 'to do' list – one day she had hoped, she and Den might afford a proper holiday. It looked unlikely now.

There were still some flights, great solar powered jets that filled the skies, but they were being phased out. The new railways were more efficient and often quicker. They also provided millions of people with employment.

Lena now wanted to check which routes were completed. She knew the European routes were finished, had seen the huge glass tunnels that connected the major cities. The trains were moved through the vacuum filled tubes at high speed, hovering over the rails, powered by electromagnets. The lack of resistance meant that the speeds produced were intense, so each carriage was sealed and oxygen filled before departing from the central stations, much like aeroplanes in the past. Lena had never travelled on a tube train but she knew about them from the online newsfeed and most of her friends had used them.

John looked up when Lena knocked and invited her in. She asked if she could use the computer, told him she was interested in the latest train routes and he nodded, called them onto his computer screen, projected them onto the wall so they could look together. He wanted to befriend Lena, felt that there might be a use for her in his plan, needed to gain her trust. So he didn't tell her that they preferred to use boats, did not ask her reasons for looking at the routes. He simply stood beside her and stared at the map.

The countries were displayed with the United Kingdom on the far left, being the easternmost point that the railways reached, though Paris was still the nearest access point for the main tube. To travel across the Atlantic, that great swathe of ocean with tides and currents that defeated human engineering, was discouraged. Those who needed to still flew. Everyone else travelled west. The nearest big rail hub to Paris was Astana in Kazakhstan - you could travel directly there. Then it was necessary to change, either to a South bound tube into Africa, down towards Australia or to the westernmost tip of Russia. There was another completed tube that ran the length of the Americas, but the link between there and Russia was still under construction. So too were the smaller, subsidiary tubes, those that would run from the main hubs to individual countries. Canada was not yet joined, the mountains proving too slow for it to be a priority. It was doubtful if the smaller islands would ever be joined, sea and air still being the best routes.

Lena frowned, crinkling her eyes so she could see better. She needed to have more laser treatment – her short-sightedness was increasing – but that would have to wait now. She traced the completed routes on the map. The best option seemed to be from Kazakhstan via a subsidiary down to Persia. Perhaps they could settle there. Would it be safe? She did not yet feel ready to share her thoughts with John, so she glanced down, saw the paper plans spread out on his desk, asked if they were from the hospital.

"Yes, that's right, they arrived this morning. Come and look." He smoothed a section, showed her the legend at the side. They were large creamy white sheets, creased where they had been folded. Lena touched the paper, gauging its texture. It was rare to see anything of importance written manually, on paper.

John pointed at a thin line. "Look, this is the plan of all the electrical wiring. It goes above the ceilings but has a crawl space, in case human repairs are necessary. Occasionally a fault can't be detected electronically, sometimes they still require humans to actually go and look."

Lena bent down and peered at the map. Faint blue lines showed the position of walls; dotted black lines showed the routes the wires had been laid along. There were red triangles which marked the position of access points. She assumed they would be hatches in the ceiling. The thought of crawling along those tunnels, suspended above the hospital wards, made her shudder. It would be horribly confined, like shuffling through a pothole.

John was searching for something. He suddenly smiled, let out a loud "Ha!" and pointed to a spot on the drawings. "Look, that is where I think the clones are probably being stored. And this point here," he moved his finger into what Lena assumed was a corridor directly outside the room, "is an access point. Look, it's really close. Perfect".

There was a tap on the door, it opened slowly and Den's head appeared.

"Hello, Agnes said I might find you here," he said to Lena. He spotted the plans and walked across. "Are these the hospital plans?"

John nodded and showed them to Den, pointing out the key, explaining the routes that were possible. He looked at Den and Lena, heads close, hair mingling together as they studied the prints. He was thinking. Which one would be best? Which one was capable physically and suitably motivated? Which one was expendable?

Den straightened and frowned. "It all looks a bit complicated," he remarked, "and dangerous. Are you sure that whoever goes in will ever find their way around? Will they manage to get out again?"

"Well," said John, considering, "I doubt it will be easy. But yes, now we have the plans we can mark a route, access the crawl space somewhere relatively private, get to above the clones. After they have been tampered with, the volunteer can escape along the same route. I'm not sure how soundproof it will be," he admitted, "if they can hear sounds from the hospital below they should assume they can also be heard. May have to avoid moving while there are people below. Might be better to go at night…"

A plan was beginning to form. John half shut his eyes, gazed at the wall, unseeing.

Den followed his gaze, saw the map projected onto the wall. "What's that for?" he asked. He moved nearer, saw it was the tube routes, the finished lines marked in blue, the hubs clearly marked, and the proposed routes dotted in, marked where the work had already begun. It was not dissimilar to the hospital plans. A blueprint on a global scale.

Lena took a deep breath, braced herself for the difficult conversation. There was no delaying it now.

"I wanted to see which routes were finished. To plan for you and the children to leave." She moved to next to him, took his hand, looked into his eyes.

"Den, I know you won't want to leave without me, but I would like to be part of this, I want to help John to get the medication. It needs to be one of us, they're using our address as cover, they will know who goes into the house. You can't do it. I know you are getting better all the time but you're not quite back yet." She paused, choosing her words, wanting to make a strong case, knowing that if she overdid it he would be angry, she would have lost the argument. "Sometimes your memory is muddled, sometimes your brain processes things more slowly than it used to. If you go back, there might be something that needs a quick decision, something unexpected. I think it should be me, not you.

"But I'm worried about the consequences. I know Nargis said the stuff would have a delayed reaction, but she can't be sure of that can she? What if it works instantly, as soon as the person injecting it reaches the clones? Or if they are captured before they get there and the plan is uncovered? What if they guess we were involved and the authorities came to the island, if it stops being a safe place? I don't want the children here then. You should take them, escape while you can. It will be easier for me to slip away, to join you later.

"Look, if you can get to Kazakhstan, then I will......"

Den pulled away from her, wrenching his hand from her grasp. Angry spots appeared in his eyes as he glared at her. "No Lena, that's not happening. I am not leaving you, not again. It's too risky.

"Tell her John," he said, turning to the elderly man, looking for support. "Lena shouldn't be the one to collect the vials."

John shook his head. "Actually Den, I think Lena is right, her plan is a good one.

"But Lena, you won't come back to the island, you should go straight away, as soon as you have administered the medication."

Lena frowned, shook her head. "But I am only collecting it from the house. I will pass it to one of your watchers. Someone else will inject the clones."

"No, I don't think that will work," John corrected her. He moved back to the computer, changed the map of tube routes for one of the town where Lena and Den lived.

"Look, here is your house. Now, I suggest that you go at night, take a car from the tunnel to your house, try to arrive around midnight. You can go in, light a few lamps, make it appear that you are staying, getting some rest before you return to the island with the medicine for Lucy. Instead, you should change into some dark clothes.

"You will then need to walk to the hospital, taking a car is too risky." His finger traced a path from her home to the hospital. "You will need to avoid being seen, keep to the shade, crouch down if a car passes. It shouldn't be too hard, no one is likely to be around at that hour.

"Then enter the hospital here, by the staff entrance. I will arrange for you to be met. They can take you here," his finger moved to another point, "to this access point near to the washrooms. You can then make your way" – he chose not to say 'crawl', he was trying to make this sound easy – "to here. Lower yourself through the corridor access point, administer the medication, return the way you came. My contact will be waiting; you can make your way home. The following morning you can order a car, leave. The authorities won't even know that you left the house." He stopped, his plan explained.

Den and Lena stared at him, incredulous. For a moment neither spoke.

Then they both said "No," together, one voice.

"That's ridiculous…" began Den.

"I couldn't do that," said Lena. "I am not some kind of athlete or special agent. I would be physically unable to do all of that, even if I wanted to. You need to find someone else. I will help collect the stuff but that is all. I am not going to that hospital. I am not doing your dirty work for you."

She was angry now, they both were. Angry and a little afraid. This scheme was far beyond their experience, seemed outrageous, impossible. They wondered if John was losing touch with reality. Lena couldn't do that, neither of them could. That was not who they were. They were just ordinary people.

They excused themselves, said they needed some space to think, went for a stroll. John watched them go. He rolled up the plans, switched off the computer, continued to think. He was not accustomed to having his plans thwarted. He would need to approach from another direction. He rested his elbows on the desk and stared at the fireplace, his eyes narrow and unseeing.

Den and Lena walked. They left the cottage and headed for the cliffs, enjoying the fresh air, the wind in their hair. They held hands, their steps in time with each other, both feeling slightly shell-shocked. That had been an unreal experience, completely unexpected. There was no way that John's plans could involve them. They were agreed. Neither of them would be going to the hospital – if that is what John was pressing for then they would leave together before this craziness began.

Their footsteps gradually slowed as their anger dissipated. Lena leant into Den and he put his arm around her shoulders. They walked towards the cliff edge, enjoying the feeling of oneness. John's unbelievable request had joined them closer than if he had tried to resolve their conflict. They had been shocked onto the same side, completely united in anger that John should consider such a thing. They began to discuss leaving the island. They were grateful for the islanders help, of course they were, but they were not about to become embroiled in some illegal resistance movement. They had the children to consider. They would return from their walk and discuss things with Agnes, she was perhaps the more rational of the two. Then they would tell the children they were leaving and pack their few possessions. If John would help them, they would leave in a boat; if not, they could walk. It was a long way but not too far, not if it meant safety for the children. They thought it unlikely that John would actually block them, arrange for the tunnel exits to be locked. He would understand that he could not force them to help him, if they were unwilling, that would be an end to the matter.

Lena was still willing to help by collecting the vials from the house. They decided they would be clear on this, it might encourage John to be more helpful about their departure. Den was unhappy that it was not himself volunteering, but he understood her objections, agreed it was a minor risk for her. Lena was still keen to be involved, just with the collecting part of the plan. She felt sure it would help her to be more star-like, to be included and accepted when it came to deciding who actually *was* a star. They strolled back to the cottage, content in each other's company, not hurrying, at peace with the world.

That is before Max was taken. Then everything changed.

Removed

For a while, no one noticed.

Lena had informed John that she was willing to collect the medication for the clones but had been adamant about bringing it to the island. Either that, or someone else would have to come directly to the house and collect it. John had accepted her help, said that it would be better, less suspicious, if Lena could return to the mainland and collect it. He would send her a message - probably a hand delivered one, letting her know what he had decided about administering it, later, when he had had time to make arrangements.

Lena had then taken Lucy aside, somewhere they were likely to be overheard, if anyone was listening, told her that she was looking pale, Lena wanted to do a health check. They had gone into the bathroom, Lena had used the cottage's health kit, checked Lucy's temperature, taken a throat swab, examined her. Everything was fine, the girl was completely healthy, but Lena had made lots of worried noises. She checked the list of symptoms that Nargis had given her, spoke each one aloud as if finding evidence of them in Lucy's medical check. Lucy stared at her, somewhat perturbed. She had felt completely well but she now began to wonder if perhaps her mother was right. Perhaps her throat was a little sore but she hadn't noticed. Perhaps she was feeling rather warm, more warm than just a little run would produce. She frowned, putting her hand to her forehead. Yes, she thought she was getting a headache too. Her mother was right, she must be ill.

Lena smiled as she watched her daughter begin to act as ill as she was being told she was. This was going to be easier than she thought. She would have to write her a note later, explaining that although she couldn't speak about it, Lucy was perfectly healthy, it was all a game. For now though, it was easier to let the child think she might be ill. She could have a few extra cuddles, some warm drinks, lap up some sympathy. It might be nice for her to enjoy a little extra attention for a few hours.

The details concerning the replica doll had arrived. Lena used her computer to photograph and measure Lucy's head. There were specific instructions about the sizing of the photographs. She used the distance program on her computer, so a tiny point of light was produced. She used this to make precise measurements, each photograph of a different angle, a set distance from Lucy's head. The girl assumed that this was connected with her illness. She began to feel very unwell indeed, never before had her mother taken such trouble over a health check.

As soon as she could, Lucy escaped to her bedroom and lay on the bed. She tested her limbs and turned her head. She was not sure, but they felt fine. She did feel a little warm. And her head did ache. She decided she must be extremely ill but also very brave and therefore not noticing. She turned on a viewing experience, a rare treat on the island and began to watch. Her health was soon the last thing on her mind.

Lena used her bar code to order both some medication for Lucy and a replica doll. She was rather excited about the doll, hoped it would be a good copy, that Lucy would love it. She deserved a treat. She smiled as she thought about her daughter becoming increasingly floppy as she had been checked, how easily she believed she must be ill. Then Lena began to prepare for her walk back to the mainland. She took a backpack, added some snacks and water, a light, some warm clothes. She would leave after lunch, the drones would deliver her packages this evening. She had not yet decided whether to return to the island later that night or stay at the

146

house. Probably the house was the better option. Much as she would miss Den, it was a long walk. Plus, she missed her home, spending a night there, probably her last night there, was attractive.

Max had spent the morning in his room, using his computer to access his online lessons. The teacher stood before his glass board explaining equations while Max fought to stay awake. When he started to attempt the set problems, he found it impossible, and had received several auto teacher prompts. Eventually, he was told to watch the lesson again. He had done so, but it hadn't helped much. He had struggled through the last few questions then shut down with relief. He knew that he should wait a few minutes, then check the marks and comments that were sent, but he really couldn't be bothered. He would check tomorrow. He knew they wouldn't be good.

Desperate for some fresh air, he grabbed some snacks from the kitchen – Lucy should have been in there in there, doing her own work, and he wondered where she was. He heard someone coming and quickly stuffed his snack into his pocket, continuing out into the garden. There was nothing to do. He wandered aimlessly for a while, threw some stones at a rock, climbed a tree and sat there, swinging his legs and frowning at the world. This island was so dull, so incredibly cut off. He hated it. He wondered what his parents were doing about leaving, surely his father was well enough to travel by now.

He lowered himself down, his back scuffing the rough bark as he went. It hurt, did nothing to improve his mood. He made his way back to the kitchen, wondering if it would be time for lunch. As he went inside he noticed something buzzing in the air above the door, must be a bee, a pretty big one. He took care to close the door behind him, hoped his bedroom window was shut. The island was full of insects, another thing he hated. He was always noticing them, buzzing around just above head height.

147

Lunch was cheese, a sort of soft, tasteless cheese. Max thought that it was made on the island from the sheep's milk. They ate it with rough bread which was, to Max's mind, much too tough. It hurt his gums to eat it and was an effort to chew. Everything on the island was an effort. They were all eating together in the kitchen, Agnes and Lena had placed the food on the table and they sat round, taking what they wanted. Every meal on the island was seen as a social occasion. Max hated it, it sometimes felt like a performance, everyone being polite to each other, the grown ups trying to find subjects to chat about that him and Lucy could join in with. It felt false. He would've eaten in his room - if he'd had one.

Lucy was chattering happily. Her online lessons had gone well that week and she was chattering about the comments she had received, the teacher had given her a merit for her short story. Lena asked what it was about, reminding her that she shouldn't write too much about the island, whispering that she shouldn't mention Den. The authorities would know where he was, they were confident of that, but no need to keep reminding them, to be noticed more than was necessary. Lucy nodded and smiled, not really listening. She was feeling much better now, had enjoyed her restful morning and was now ready to go outside again.

"Can I go to the beach after lunch? Can we make sand houses?" Perhaps as she was ill, her father might come and play too. She knew her mother was going to collect her medicine but her father made better sand houses anyway.

"Sorry little one, I don't have time to come with you," said Den, wanting to talk further with John, to plan their travel. There was no need to stay here any longer, it would be better to leave as soon as they could, perhaps tomorrow, when Lena returned. He knew that John preferred to use the boats, felt their routes were less easy to monitor, but Lena would prefer the tube lines. Den didn't

148

know which was safer, which was most likely to get his family away from England, away from the island. He knew that most of Asia had less strict laws, would care less about his own beliefs. He was not classed as a security threat, it was unlikely he would be stopped. He was beginning to prefer Lena's plan himself. Certainly the tubes would be more comfortable.

"I'll go with you," Max told Lucy, "but I'm not staying all afternoon. I want to read something, I'll bring it with me." That would let her know he was not going to be building any stupid sandcastles. He would go because he had nothing better to do, and he knew she wasn't allowed to go on her own. He pushed back his chair, the wooden legs scraping the tiles with a loud rasp. "In fact, I'll go down now, wait for you." He knew she would take ages getting ready, would probably want to change her clothes or something. She was always changing her clothes and checking her appearance in the mirror on the stairs. Like anyone was going to be noticing. He reached out for his computer, shoved it deep into his pocket.

"I'll wait in the little cove? The first one you get to." He nodded at his parents and left.

Immediately after lunch, Lena too left the cottage. She kissed Den and Lucy, held them for a long while, then took her bag and walked to the cave. She was slightly nervous, wanted to get the job done, but didn't expect it to be anything other than a lot of walking and rather lonely. She was also looking forward to seeing the house again.

Max walked along the path to the beach. He could feel his computer in his pocket, a comfortable weight against his leg, like an old friend. He was reading a story, set in the past in China. It was full of ninjas and tribal wars. The scenes were far removed from his own life, full of tensions and violence and strange views about loyalty towards one's own tribes. The bits he liked best described the battles, flying swordsmen and generals planning strategy. It was exciting.

The day was warm and he pulled off his sweater as he walked, wound it around his shoulders. He wondered how long Lucy would be. He scanned the beach when he arrived. It was always deserted, littered with seaweed and shells. There was a rock fairly near the path, he would sit next to that, could lean against it, use his sweater as a cushion. He lowered himself down, leaned back. It was quite comfortable and sheltered from the wind. He listened to the waves crashing onto the shore, a steady swoosh of tumbling shingle being dragged back before the next wave hit. The waves were calm today, very few white caps out to sea. He watched a boat; he assumed it was fishing, not far from the shore. Gulls screamed overhead. It was not, he decided, a bad place to spend a couple of hours reading. He changed the light setting on his screen so the reflections from the sun didn't interfere with the words, settled back and began to relax into the web of fantasy.

Something buzzed behind his head. He looked up from his screen, annoyed to be disturbed. He caught sight of something small and very fast, reached out to swot it, felt a sting on his leg. He jumped up. Something had stung him. He started to look around for it, searching for the bee or insect that had hurt him, angry, intent on squashing it. He couldn't see it. Couldn't see anything clearly in fact. His eyes were fuzzy and he wiped them on the back of his sleeve, couldn't clear his vision. He sat down, feeling dizzy, disoriented, very sleepy. He wondered if he was allergic to bee stings. It was the last thing he thought before he slid sideways and lay on the soft sand.

#

When Lucy arrived at the cove it was empty. She stood still at the end of the pathway, gazing left and right, searching for her brother. Dumping her spades and containers on the dune, she marched over to the rocks, looked behind them, returned to the dunes, scanned the beach. He was nowhere. There were some gulls, worrying something washed ashore, arguing loudly, jumping and pecking. There was a boat on the sea, a long way off, getting ever smaller as it went further from the island. There was sand and shingle, and wide blue sky with grey clouds on the horizon. But there was no Max.

Lucy sighed. She thought about stamping her foot, decided she was too old for that now. Where was he? Lucy was not supposed to go to the beach on her own. She was not quite sure what her mother was worried about, probably she thought Lucy would attempt to swim on her own and be swept out to sea or something. Something that a little girl might do. Her mother hadn't noticed that Lucy was not a little girl, she was quite old now and very sensible. She liked the beach, liked the whole island in fact. Her parents had more time here, they played with her more often, read to her sometimes. They didn't laugh much – Lucy knew they were worried about something – but apart from the fact that her and Max had to share a room, she was perfectly happy.

Max was sometimes annoying, tended to tease her, but mostly he was kind, helped with her online schoolwork, smuggled sugary food from the kitchen when no one was looking, and shared it with her. Now he was supposed to be on the beach with her. What was she going to do? She knew what she ought to do, she ought to go back to the cottage, carrying all her things, which had made her fingers sore on the way here. She ought to go back and tell Den that Max had lied, he wasn't here. There was a chance her father would feel sorry for her, perhaps come back with her, he made the best sand towns. But she knew that was unlikely. Her parents had been preoccupied at lunch, sharing glances, their thoughts on other things. Lucy knew that he would tell her to play at the cottage, to find something else to do.

Lucy was not a little girl, she was not going to swim on her own, or get lost, or be suddenly afraid of monsters. She was quite capable of playing safely on the beach on her own. She would do that. She would build a sand town, do what she had come to do. Then she would return to the cottage. If she found Max first, perhaps they could make a deal, pretend he had been with her all the time, then neither of them would be in trouble. If her father saw her first, then she would explain what had happened, that it was not her fault, she had been abandoned. Maybe they would realise she was older than they thought after all, maybe they would allow her to come on her own in future. She hoped so.

It was a good plan; so she carried her containers to a better spot, where the sand was moist but not too wet, before the shingle started, knelt down and began to build. She started to hum a tune, heaving mounds of sand into a pot, pressing it down with her fingers. Thus ensuring that no one realised Max was missing for several hours.

#

The person responsible for taking Max was known as Mel4. She worked for England security and had been reviewing the family's files for a few days. Most of the work in the department was done by the bots, a network of intelligent computers, but everything needed to be checked by a human. Not because they were more reliable than the bots, but because they were not. A few decades ago, all decision-making was done by bots. They could input data and make decisions much faster than a human and could then instigate action almost immediately.

The problems had arisen due to human error. If someone entered the wrong codes originally, perhaps marked someone as high risk when actually they weren't, then it was not always noticed and corrected before the network actioned a response. There had been embarrassing incidents when officials had been detained, or admitted to hospital, simply because the wrong codes had been entered, the slip of a finger or a tired human mind. The bots were efficient but did not notice anomalies, they assumed everything they were given was correct. Bots do not lie, or make mistakes and they did not have the capacity to notice when their human co-workers did.

So now, although most data processing was done by the bots, human overseers checked anything unusual. No serious action was taken, no permissions given or denied without regular human checks.

Mel4 was tired. She had spent the last two days reading the files relating to the island, much of it transcripts of conversations collected by the listening drones. The island was a problem, one she would have liked to ignore. But it could not be ignored any longer.

Mel4 had read the conversation between the two men on the cliff. She knew that it was likely the boy had accessed room 273, had told the island group something of what he had seen. That constituted a national security threat. They had no data that showed he had actually given them details, but the bots had sanctioned acting anyway. They had advised he should be altered. It was much easier to deny things if there were no witnesses, and the boy would cease to be a witness if altered.

Taking a child was rare and extreme. It was not something they often did, not something they would ever want made public. Usually pressure on the parents was sufficient to control minors; it was rare that a child needed treatment themselves. Mel4 had children herself, she was uneasy with the conclusions of the bots. A machine had no feelings, was not swayed by emotion. That could be both a strength and, in her view, a weakness.

Clearly some action needed to be taken and quickly. Mel4 had sanctioned the removal of the boy from the island. That would buy her some time. She would decide what to do tomorrow, she was too tired now. She was waiting for confirmation that the boy had been safely delivered to the hospital, was unharmed. Then she would go home. She was hungry, needed to eat something, have a hot bath, relax with a viewing experience. She hoped her husband had planned something easy for dinner, something she could eat without thinking.

The screen in front of her blinked and she leaned forwards. There were details of the boy's removal. Good, nothing had gone wrong. She scanned the medical report, frowning when she read that his back was grazed. That should not have happened, she would follow that up in the morning, find out why. The team sent to the island was experienced; there should not have been injuries.

She stretched her back, raised her arms towards the ceiling and yawned. She really was too tired to do this now. She entered a stalling code into the bot. The boy would be safe enough at the hospital, could be kept sedated for a few hours. He could be watched remotely just in case, but she wanted no further action until she had decided it was necessary, decided what would happen next. The bots would advise her, but it was up to her whether to follow that advice.

Tomorrow there was a function; Midra was due to speak to some delegates from North America. This would usually have been done electronically but they were in England, visiting as part of a global tour, and Midra had decided to meet them in person. Mel4 needed to check the security arrangements, see that everything was in place for a peaceful visit. There was very little crime in the country, the hormones in the water and the altering of anyone considered a threat had seen to that. But complacency was inexcusable. There was the occasional aberration and it was her job to think ahead, to avoid any incidents.

She looked at her screen. The bot was speaking, telling her the arrangements for Midra but she couldn't listen. The voice, although varied in tone, was obviously simulated and she found it slightly irritating.

"Be quiet. I'll read the reports," she told it. At least with a bot you could be blunt, rude even, say what you wanted. The bot hooted an acknowledgement and whirred into the corner where it sat, round and squat like a black tub, waiting for her next instruction.

Midra was due to arrive at the holy place at twelve noon. Holy places were often used for meetings, being one of the few large halls that still existed in most towns. There was limited use for large crowds to meet, everything was so much easier to view online, and the Global Council had tried to limit large crowds, as they were also viewed as possible security risks. There were still sports stadiums and concert halls, but the price of attending was very high, only a select few could afford to go. An elite few. Which was how the Council liked it. These elite were rigorously screened, their every word, almost their every thought was monitored. They were considered completely non-risk, could even apply to be Council members themselves one day, if the need ever arose.

Midra would arrive in his own car, which was armoured to a high specification, no risk there. The car would park under an awning, so it would not be possible to see from above when Midra left the car. He would enter the building by a side door, surrounded by guards, both human and bots, who would also fill the front and back row of seats in the holy place. He would meet the delegates, say a few words, the cameras would record him shaking hands, then he would leave. The visit would be very brief, an air-kiss really, no actual physical contact. Then he would be away, back to the safety of his work station. Mel4 couldn't foresee any problems.

155

She was after all, only human. A very tired human who now wanted her dinner.

Standing, she moved away from the terminal. Tomorrow, she decided, it could all be sorted tomorrow.

Chapter Nine

The Puppeteer

Den walked towards the beach, going to meet Lucy and Max. He was feeling better than he had for weeks, optimistic and hopeful.

They would pack tonight and leave early tomorrow morning, as soon as Lena returned. They would ask John about taking a boat to the mainland but if he refused to help they would walk through the tunnel. He hoped Lena would have the energy for another walk but he thought she would, the adrenaline would spur her on. They would then take a car straight to London, take a train to Paris. There they could join the completed tube line and travel to Kazakhstan, then onwards to Asia. It would be exciting, an adventure. They both felt there was almost no risk of being detained, the local governments would be happy to see them leave, the Asians ones would view their immigration as routine, a normal move to seek new work.

They had decided to tell John that evening, either when Lena returned or if she decided to stay, then when Den had heard from her, knew that she had arrived safely.

Neither option happened. When Den finally went in search of John it was to tell him that Max was missing.

Den had seen Lucy as soon as he arrived at the cove. She was playing near the water's edge, diligently filling her containers, emptying them in turn. As he drew nearer he could see the damp sand staining her trousers, globs of it stuck to her hair, filling her nails. She was completely absorbed by her task, lost in her own world, happy. He smiled. Then he looked for Max and frowned. Where was he?

When he reached Lucy she looked up with a sandy grin, which faded to uncertainty as she remembered that she was alone. She blurted her story before Den had even asked, explained that Max had lied, it wasn't her fault, she had decided to wait for him to arrive, she didn't know where he was. Den was mildly amused by her protestations of innocence, he decided to humour her, keen to avoid a cross confrontation. He had calmly observed that she should have returned to the cottage, then suggested that perhaps neither of them need mention this to Lena. Lucy had grinned then, realising he was agreeing to be complicit in her plan. They had gathered her things, rinsed them in the sea, admired her structures. Neither of them hurried, both assuming that Max had changed his mind, was safely reading somewhere else.

It wasn't until Den had walked to the next cove and scanned the cliffs, that he began to worry. Lucy was beside him, chattering about her sand town, explaining how the stream was an integral part of her design. Den barely heard her, something uncomfortable forming in his stomach, a sense of dread beginning to dawn. He hurried Lucy back to the cottage, searching as they walked. Then they looked in the garden, the sheds, the cottage. It became ever more certain that Max was missing. Den realised that he could be on a different part of the island, that he might have walked to the harbour, or found a cave to read in, or a thousand other possibilities. But inside, he knew. When he could delay it no longer, he went to tell John.

John listened to Den. How he had searched the beach and the cottage, walked along the cliff top, but found no trace of him. He saw the panic in Den's eyes, held in check by a glimmer of hopefulness, knew that he was wondering if John was tracking him, if it was a repeat of his disappearance before, when he had set off to rescue his father. Maybe he was following his mother this time. But John could not help, he had no idea where the boy was. He went to his computer and sent some messages, asking for watchers at the guesthouse and church, just in case the boy had used the tunnel. Den watched him, sensing that John was 'going through the motions', behaving in an expected manner, but perhaps not really anticipating success. Did John know more than he was sharing? The thought was brief, barely noticed before it was gone, but it left Den uneasy. He left and went to the cottage he shared with Lena, needing to be alone for a moment, to make some decisions.

John continued through his list of contacts, though he suspected they would draw blanks. He thought that he knew where the boy would be, would have been taken. It was not information he would share with the father. Not until he had confirmation. Not until he had had time to think.

Den knew that the boy was not on the island, he felt it inside, knew that he had been taken. He prayed, kneeling in his room, beseeching God to keep their boy safe. His mind was full of the hospital, wondering if they would take Max there. He could almost smell the detergent, see the glare of the lights, feel the fear as they injected him with another chemical, as he woke from another operation, as all control was taken from him. Nothing had ever been explained, he was an animal in a science laboratory, a specimen to be examined. Now he worried his son might be there. What Den had suffered was hard to bear, the thought of someone he loved suffering the same fate was almost too much. He felt lost, powerless, frustrated with the slowness of his brain. It seemed so long since they had left their home, since everything was normal. Den realised how precious 'normal' was, how little he had appreciated it before life began to change.

Then he returned to the kitchen. Agnes had served large plates of steaming pasta and vegetables. Lucy was watchful, wondering if she was in trouble, worried that they had not found Max. She thought he had probably gone back through the tunnel, gone to collect something from the house or to see his friends. She wondered if he had a girlfriend, she knew some of his friends had. She thought he would probably be in trouble this time when he returned to the island, would not receive the same welcome he had before. Which she supposed served him right for abandoning her, for not being on the beach when he had promised to be.

Den stirred his food, unable to eat. Even the water tasted sour in his mouth. He was trying to appear calm, to keep up an appearance of normality for Lucy, but inside he was a wreck. His wife on her way to the mainland, their son goodness knows where, and Den felt like he was in a dream, a nightmare that was spiralling out of control. When Lucy had finished eating, he told her she should stay inside, read or play a game. He wanted to keep her safe, though could not say that without worrying her. Then he went into the sitting room and sat, his leg twitching, staring at the window with unseeing eyes. He wanted to do something, to follow Lena through the tunnel, to tell her about Max and to begin searching for him. But he knew that they were right, that though his brain was better it was still often fuzzy, that he would be a liability rather than a help. He had to trust others to find his son, to keep his wife safe. "Let them be safe God," he prayed, over and over, like a mantra in his head.

#

Max *was* safe, but sleepy, so very sleepy. His head felt very heavy and when he tried to lift it he found that he couldn't. He was aware that his mouth was open, and he shut it. He could hear someone in the room with him but opening his eyes was too much effort. He wondered if he was dreaming, then drifted back to sleep.

#

Lena arrived at the house to a note fastened to the inside of the front door, where she could not fail to notice it. She wondered who had gained access to her house, how they had bypassed the security. That thought disappeared as soon as she read the note. She sank to her knees, the hard floor smacking into her joints.

The message was brief: Max is missing. Den went to meet him and Lucy from the beach but only Lucy was there, Lucy said Max had never arrived. They had searched the island but were confident that he was not there, was gone. Lena should wait at the house until they had more information.

The message was unsigned.

#

In another room, in another building, Mel4 was reading her reports, trying to check that the arrangements for Midra were secure. She still needed to make a decision regarding the boy, knew that she couldn't delay for much longer. But Midra was her priority.

#

John received news of Max. He went to find Den.

"I've had some news. Max is in the hospital. Do you want to read the email?"

Den followed John back into the study. John projected the email onto the wall and they stood, staring at it. It was very short.

"J. We have news of the boy. X2 found his admission papers in hospital 05. He appears to have been taken. Unharmed. Sedated but no treatment to date. Awaiting instruction. P4."

Den sank into a chair. "What does that mean? Taken? And where is hospital 05? Is that near the island?"

"It means," said John, "that they must have taken him from the beach. They probably used drones to sedate him and then carried him onto a boat. He will be okay, they won't have hurt him".

He paused, then went to the computer and stooping over the keyboard began to write:

"We should write rather than speak, we do not know who is listening. They must have discovered he went to the room with the clones. Possibly overheard conversation. My guess is they will alter him in some way, try to make him forget about the room, about what he saw. Then he will either be returned to the island or taken to another place to live, hard to guess what they'll do.

"Hospital 05 is the one in your town, where you were treated. It has the most advanced neurosurgery, so it makes sense. It is also, ironically, where the clones are."

Den read as John wrote, barely breathing. He reached forwards and wrote:

"We have to get him back. I will go and get him."

John frowned, shook his head. He sat in his chair, pulled the keyboard towards him and began to type. He told Den that he was not mentally well enough to make the trip, he must allow Lena to go to the hospital. His watchers would help her, she would not be alone. She could rescue Max and return to the island. He would have a boat waiting that could take the whole family to Paris and then they could get a tube train, travel further into Europe.

They both knew that once they had left England, the authorities would mark them as low priority. Each country had their own security departments. They worked together, as a unified globe, when there was a major threat to security. The family's beliefs did not come into that category. Only Midra pursued religious faith with such force.

John did *not* write that his help depended on her administering the medication for the clones. He put no conditions on her at all. That would come later, when she was in the hospital, when she would not be in a position to refuse. This plan was important, more important than the mental health of one boy. But he did not expect the parents to appreciate that, especially not the mother. No, it was a fair trade, his help in keeping her boy safe, for her help in changing the world for the better. Sometimes it was best to impart information slowly, to not allow too much thought, too many choices. He had learnt that long ago. It was why he could make things happen. It was why he was such a proficient puppeteer.

#

In her home on the mainland, Lena was sitting in her lounge, a viewing experience flickering on the screen, her eyes closed. She could barely contain her anxiety but until she knew where Max was, there was nothing she could do. On her lap were the parcels the drones had delivered. She had opened the smaller box, the one containing the medication for Lucy's invented illness, and a tiny package, filled with goodness knows what, intended for the clones. She didn't even want to touch it, even though she was sure it would be properly sealed. The other box, the larger one, remained unopened. Lena knew it contained a replica doll, knew it was likely to be a very accurate copy of her daughter, knew that if she saw that face she would break down completely. She needed to remain strong, suspend all emotion for now. She needed to rescue her son.

There was a sound at the door and she jumped up. She carried the clone parcel with her, unsure if this was simply a courier, someone who had come to collect the vials, or a person who could tell her where her son was. She opened the door and a man pushed his way inside. He held up a hand when she started to speak, indicated that she shouldn't. He then took his computer and began to write, holding it so that Lena could see. She peered over his shoulder, feeling his rough coat on her chin, squinting so she could read the words.

"Please do not speak, they might be listening. Your son is at hospital 05, the one in this town. You must go and collect him and take him to the island. Someone will meet you there to help you. Do not order a car, you need to walk there, I will leave you with a

163

paper map. You should assume everything on the internet is monitored. Wear dark clothing, keep to the shadows. Rest first, you will be met at 8am. The walk should take you one hour. When you arrive, go to this entrance," he indicated on the map. There was a large red cross, like on a child's treasure map. *"The person meeting you will tell you what to do next. You should take everything with you, you will not return to the house. Take the clone medication, that is a priority."* He looked up, checked that Lena had read that sentence. She nodded, yes, she understood.

The man passed her the map, shut off his computer, then took her hand. He stared at her. It felt like a test. Lena stared back, not sure what he was trying to convey, not sure if he was trying to help her or was making sure she understood the instructions, what they wanted her to do. His eyes were blue, and very intense as he looked at her. Lena found it uncomfortable, lowered her gaze. He released her hand, nodded and departed.

Lena closed the door behind him and locked it. She felt slightly sick and completely exhausted but in a wound-up, not-able-to-sleep way. She went back to the lounge and sat for a moment, trying to order her thoughts. Part of her couldn't quite believe this was happening, felt as if she would wake from a nightmare any minute. She wanted to crawl into bed, pull the covers over her head, stay there until it was all over. But she knew that it would not be over, not until she had rescued her son. She was the only one who could finish it, there was no one else.

She checked the time. It was late evening now, still a long time until 8am. She recognised that she was tired but would be unable to sleep, however the practical part of her brain knew that she should restock her energy, that if she was going to collect Max she needed to have some resources. She would force herself to eat and rest, even if sleep eluded her.

First, she altered the climate control in the house, she was cold. Then she walked to the kitchen, comforted by the familiarity of her home. She wanted wine but poured juice into a glass, drank it, willed the sugar to give her energy. Then she slid open the freezer draw, wished she had stocked it with more meals, assumed that using her bar code was inadvisable. If they had taken Max, perhaps they would take her too. She didn't know if they had followed her plan to return to the mainland, had heard her pretend conversations, thought that Lucy was ill; or if all that had been in vain. The only thing she did know was that she should be careful, the authorities were proving unpredictable, she shouldn't take any chances. She wondered fleetingly if she should go somewhere else, if even staying in the house was taking a risk. But where would she go? No, she decided she was probably safer staying there, it was only a few hours. She checked the time again.

She pulled some sandwiches from the freezer, put them to defrost, boiled some water, made some tea. Then she carried her meal to the table, sat where Max had sat a few weeks before, forced herself to eat. Each mouthful was like eating sawdust but she was hungry, her body absorbed the food, she ate it all. Checked the time again. It was moving very slowly, six hours before she could leave.

Lena cleared her meal, put the dishes to wash. She wasn't sure why really, if they never returned to the house, did it matter if it was left messy? But somehow she couldn't bring herself to ignore the mess; she wanted to leave the house clean and tidy. She checked the time, then went upstairs to shower.

She touched the dial by the door as she entered the bathroom and the shower turned on, the sound comforting. Steam billowed from the screen and she removed her clothes, slid it open, walked under the spray. The water relaxed her, the white noise helping to calm her thoughts. She looked through the steam at the mess of the children, plastic toys and half-finished soap bottles.

Some people had two bathrooms, but only the very rich. Some older houses had been built with them, an ensuite for the master bedroom, sometimes for each room. But they were a taxable luxury, considered an excessive use of space in an overpopulated planet. Most people had converted them back to rooms, living in houses that had no more than the required number of rooms for their family size. Spare bedrooms were another taxable luxury, one that her and Den had paid until Lucy was born, until their family fitted their house size.

She turned a dial, changing the water to air; stood beneath the warm vents, drying, enjoying the warmth for a moment before stepping out, walking to her room. She opened her cupboards. Dark clothes. She felt like a second rate spy in a cheap viewing experience. She chose her clothes and pulled them on. Checked the time. Still hours to wait. She lay on the bed, her hair still damp. It was soft, welcoming, supported her tense body, willed her to relax. Her eyes closed. She did not sleep but she lay, as if dead, for three hours, resting her limbs if not her mind.

At 6am she rose, ate, then packed her bag. She carried the clone medication and the doll. Taking the doll was foolish she knew, but she wanted it, wanted a prize for having come. And her mind was too tired for rational thought so she packed it, still in its box, at the bottom of her bag. When she swung it onto her back she could feel the edges of the box digging into her ribs. The medicine for Lucy she left; discarded on a shelf, its usefulness finished. She took a long look around the room, walked to the hall and opened the door. The street was deserted, the early morning air crisp and clean. She stepped outside and pulled the door to her home shut behind her.

To the Hospital

Lena walked away from the house. She didn't bother to look for electronic watchers, she knew she wouldn't see them anyway. She kept to the shadows, hugging the side of a wall, walking so close to a bush the thorns caught her elbow, brushing the side of buildings as she passed.

It was cold. Lena could see her breath in puffs of condensed air, coming quickly as she hurried towards the hospital. A car passed her, then another. Neither slowed and she didn't look at them, was almost past caring if she was seen. This whole experience was too foreign, too unreal, like being caught up in a psychological thriller.

When she reached the corner opposite the old school, she stopped and leant forwards, resting her hands on her knees. She had a pain in her side, knew she was walking too fast to be comfortable, faster than someone with her level of fitness could maintain. She had a long way to go, was still tired from the walk through the tunnel. When she straightened the world spun briefly, a haze of grey and brown. Then her vision cleared, she took some deep breaths, forced herself to calm her breathing, to relax her shoulders. Another car was approaching, its lights sweeping the road, the faint whir of its motor audible in the silence of the early morning. Lena continued walking.

There were lights on in most of the houses, casting a cheery glow into the grey morning. Lena longed to go to them, to knock on a door, ask for help. She could see people inside, preparing to leave for work, eating with their families, chatting, happy, normal, living within the bounds of the law. She wondered how she had got here, what had led her to this place of unwanted adventure and fear, wondered if she could have avoided it.

By the time she got near to the hospital, her legs were aching and the strap of her bag dug cruelly into her shoulders. She wondered if she would have a blister. Certainly she had one on her left heel, the skin was sore and her shoe rubbed painfully. She stopped, moving her sock, trying to alleviate the pressure slightly. When she looked up, she could see the hospital, shining on the hill like a beacon. It seemed every room was lit, it sat there, a glowing fat spaceship, watching over the valley.

The road up to the hospital was lined with trees and Lena walked amongst them, following the line of the road but away from it, hoping to remain unseen. It was fully daylight now and there was a steady stream of cars to and from the hospital, carrying patients, staff, visitors. She tripped on a raised root and staggered, got her balance, continued, taking better care to look where she was going.

She checked the map she had been given, the one showing where she would be met. There was an entrance on the right hand side of the hospital, a narrow driveway led to it, with a circle for the cars to turn, drop their passengers and leave. She checked the time, she was early. Not wanting to stand on the driveway where she might be seen she turned, walked deeper into the trees. There was a small clearing and she sat on the moss, leaned against a trunk. The ground was damp, the moisture almost instantly seeping upwards, through her trousers. She really could not be bothered to move. She reached into her bag, pulled out an energy biscuit and ate it, crumbs falling on the ground and scattering across her jacket. Absently she wiped them away, then took a look at her heel. It was sore but not blistered. She dug out a tissue, tried to pad the heel of her sock. It hurt. She checked the time. It was moving slowly now. She waited.

At 8am, Lena walked from the trees onto the driveway. A couple of cars passed her, people hurried out and into the building; no one seemed to notice her, to wonder why she was walking. She approached the door, uncertain. A nurse saw her, came out. He did not speak, just walked towards the woods, back to where she had come from, indicated for her to follow.

When they were back in the trees, mostly hidden from the road he stopped.

"Hello, w-i-n-d-e-n473?" he asked, using the beginning of her bar code.

She nodded, glanced at his own bar code. The colour bands showed he was highly educated, a senior nurse, owned a small property, had no family. He nodded back at her.

"Good, you are on time, well done."

He passed her a different bar code, the plastic slightly worn, the pin behind it twisted. "Wear this. It belongs to another watcher, another nurse. It will be picked up by the scanners, they will assume she is arriving for work. I have her uniform," he looked at Lena, appraising her size, body shape. She felt herself redden under his scrutiny.

"I think it will fit you. I will take you to a washroom, you can change there. You have the vials?"

Lena frowned, not sure what he meant, then realised he was referring to the package for the clones. She nodded, lifted the box from her back, offered it to him.

The nurse shook his head. "No, you keep them. When you have changed, put your clothes in the bag but keep the vials. We can stow your things in the ceiling, I will show you. Then I will take you to the access hatch and help you in. Here," he passed her a piece of paper.

Lena unfolded it. It was another map, a maze of lines, crosses marked at intervals. She had seen it before. It was the map that John had shown her in the cottage, the one that showed where the wiring routes were.

"Why are you showing me this?" Lena was confused, then alarmed as she realised what he was assuming. "No, no, I'm not doing this. I have come for my son. I was told you would help me." She backed away, her back touched the trunk of a tree and she stood there, staring at him, confused. What was happening? Why was he saying these strange things? She had come to find Max, to take him away, they had said they would help her.

The nurse raised his hands, placating. "Keep calm, breathe, it's okay, I *am* helping you," he said, seeing the rising hysteria, needing her calm, sane. "We are going to get Max, you are going to take him away, to somewhere safe." His voice was low, slow, willing her to trust him. He looked at her. Her hair was tangled, sticking to her wet forehead, her eyes, red-rimmed from lack of sleep and worry. She stood, slumped against the tree trunk, exhausted, defeated. He seriously doubted she was up to this. But she was all they had. And time was running out. He needed to be back on shift in twenty minutes or his absence would be noticed. She needed to be in the ceiling by then, clear on what her mission entailed.

But first he must calm her, get her to rest and eat a little, persuade her to trust him. He was cross with himself; he had done this all wrong, started in the wrong place. He blamed it on the lack of time, the urgency of the situation.

"Look at me," he told her.

She looked. He was tall and strong, the white uniform stretched across his muscles. His eyes were dark, grave, hypnotic in their intensity.

"We are going to get Max," he repeated. "You are going to take him away, somewhere safe. He is safe now, no one has hurt him. We know where he is, we are watching him, checking him. But before we can take him, we need a distraction. We need to move the security staff away, to another part of the hospital. I cannot do that. You can. It will be easy. You will go to where the clones are. You will administer the injections, you will leave. If anyone sees you, they will think you are a nurse, no one will stop you. When you return, I will have Max, the staff watching him will have been called away, to where the clones are, away from where Max is. You will take Max and leave. It will be okay. Can you do that Lena?" He remembered her name now, had seen it on the report from John, hoped using it would make him more believable, a friend. "Can you do that? Can you create a diversion so that I can get Max?"

Lena nodded. Actually, she did not think she could do it. She thought she was too tired, too muddled, too frightened. But something about the way he said it, the intensity of his eyes, her lack of alternative options, made her nod. She had no choice, not really. She couldn't find Max on her own, she needed them to help her. If she did see Max, if she spotted him somewhere while they were in the hospital, then she would take him, she would leave. Their plan meant nothing to her, she had done her bit, she had collected the vials, she owed them nothing. But until she actually knew where her son was, she had no choice, she would do what this man was asking. If she could.

He lifted her bag from where she had let it fall on the mud, frowned. "Why is it so heavy?" He felt inside, asked, "What's this?"

"It's a replica doll. I bought it for my daughter."

"And you thought it would be a good idea to bring it along?" he said, raising an eyebrow.

Lena was suddenly angry. What right did this man have to challenge her decisions? If she wanted to bring a doll, a gift for her child, who was he to ridicule her, to make her feel silly?

"Yes," she said, refusing to explain further.

He noted her anger, saw the fight in her, decided she might stand a chance after all.

"Come, we are running late. I will take you somewhere you can change. Then I will bring you something to eat, you need some energy. I will help you on your way before I return to work." He passed her the bag, strode away, back to the hospital.

Lena struggled to fasten the bar code to her jacket then hurried after him, avoiding roots and sticks, not wanting to be left behind. If she was stopped at the entrance, she wanted this man with her. He could explain why she was there, he was less tired than she was.

She was not stopped at the entrance. It was a staff entrance. She walked through the haze of sterilising mist with other workers, returning to their wards and offices. Her nurse, as she thought of him, strode ahead, not looking at her, not waiting for her. She followed him along bright corridors, wondering if anyone would notice her muddy boots, her damp trousers. No one appeared to, everyone was focused on where they were going, walking quickly with purpose, aware only of the time and not wanting to be late.

They came to a washroom and he slipped inside. She followed. Like all public washrooms, it was designed for both genders, with secure cubicles inside for privacy but with a shared sink area with mirrors above. Flashing signs reminded her to wash her hands, to not place bags on the floor. He told her to lean against the door, so no one else could enter, then reached up, removed a panel from the ceiling. He lowered the white tile, revealing a hole, reached inside and pulled down a bag. He passed it to Lena, then replaced the tile, clicking it into place.

"There's a uniform in there. Go into a cubicle and put it on. Make sure the door is locked and stay there until I get back."

"Where are you going?" she said, not sure she wanted to be left alone but also grateful he wouldn't be there when she changed.

"To get you something to eat." He turned and left.

Lena went into a cubicle and locked the door, lowered the lid of the toilet and sat, her head buried in her hands. The day had gone from nightmare to surreal.

She looked in the bag. The uniform, of course, was white. Lena felt very grubby after her long sweaty hike and rest in the woods. She left both bags in the cubicle and went back to the sinks, hoped no one would come in. She held her hands under the tap, waited for the flow of soapy water, washed her face, scooped the warm liquid onto her face and neck. Then she stood next to the drier, angled it to dry her face, enjoyed the warm air as it tickled her hair, chasing wisps across her forehead and neck.

She heard footsteps and hurried back into her cubicle, locked the door. Someone came in, used the cubicle next to her. She felt an insane urge to laugh, made worse by the need to keep completely silent. She sat there, not moving, hardly even breathing, trying to not listen as they used the toilet. She waited, heard them leave, wash their hands, go back into the corridor.

She pulled the clothes from the bag. There were the white trousers and tunic that all the female nurses wore, with white plastic shoes. She struggled from her own clothes, stuffing them into the bag, then dressed in the uniform. It was tight across her stomach but not noticeably so. The shoes were a bad fit, very uncomfortable but she could get them on. They squeezed her toes and pushed against her sore heel. She would not be able to walk far in them. She used her fingers to comb her hair, then refastened it in the elastic band she had. She doubted she looked very tidy but was loath to return to the mirrors now she was in uniform, unsure if this was a staff-designated washroom or intended for the public.

She rested the bag of clothes on her muddy boots on the floor, then sat back on the toilet seat. She wondered how long she would have to wait, how long before the nurse returned, how long before she had saved her son.

The Puppet Dance

Max stirred. He could hear the soft fluttering of someone moving in his room. Eyes heavy, he opened them a crack, looked out. The

173

world was bleary and white, harsh, he closed them again. The someone moved closer, he smelt almonds, felt a machine on his neck. It whirred and hummed as it measured his temperature, heartbeat, fluid levels. Then another prick, sharp, in his thigh.

"Another bee," he thought, "way too many insects," before he floated back to sleep.

#

Mel4 was back in her office. She sipped the bitter coffee in her hand, stared at the screen. She could see Midra leaving his underground garage, the car flanked by two others. The glass was black but she knew he was inside, accompanied by a human guard, with a bot fastened to the ceiling. The bot would be monitoring all passing traffic, anything unusual. The human guard would be armed. She switched to an inside monitor, all was as expected.

All human guards carried firearms, tiny guns that could shoot either instant tranquillisers or, more rarely, lethal bullets designed to kill. Neither guaranteed the immediate removal of danger as it depended on the aim of the marksman where the target was hit. There had been calls for the rearming of bots. Mel4 hoped that would never happen. She remembered too well the mistakes of the past, the malfunctioning bots who had killed innocent bystanders, the over-diligent bots who had removed enemies they would rather have interviewed. It was still too difficult to write code that tempered absolute obedience, that would enable bots to balance more than the physical elements of the situations they were in. Humans, though unreliable, were still considered more reliable than bots when it came to weapons. They were still able to weigh up situations and vary their decisions accordingly. There were fewer absolutes in the human mind, more variables. For ten years now, security bots had been armed only with sedatives, ones that worked fairly instantly but were never fatal.

174

She took another sip, then rested her cup on the desk. She would need to move that if her boss came, the roaming bot that floated around the corridors checking workers, sending instructions to her terminal. Liquids and machines were not a good mix, despite all the manufacturer's assurances that computers were watertight. She would be careful. It had been a long week, she needed the caffeine. She read through the data that had arrived so far. The holy place was secure; the delegates were on their way. They would be met by Midra at 9am, they would nod, smile, make meaningless speeches, then Midra could return to his safe bunker and the delegates could leave, knowing their importance had been acknowledged.

Her next job would be to make a decision on the boy from the island.

#

Lena was standing in an inspection room with the nurse. He had locked the door, moved the trolley bed to under a hatch in the ceiling and smoothly climbed onto it. He was now unscrewing the clips, lowering the metal plate. Lena was watching. Did he really expect her to climb up there? To shuffle through tunnels? She fingered the borrowed bar code clipped onto her borrowed uniform. She felt her feet, pinched by the borrowed shoes. She wondered if she would need to use the toilet before she got back. Heroes in stories never used toilets, she had noticed that. Women with children did though and the nurse had made her drink a lot, watched her swallow every drop of the sweet liquid, told her the fluids and sugar would do her good.

She glanced down at the map in her hand. She had nearly forgotten to bring it, had left it in the side pocket of her bag. He had reminded her, raised that eyebrow again, suggested it might be useful unless she had committed it to memory. His sarcasm was irritating, made her want to slap him.

175

He had finished removing the hatch and he sat on the bed, holding it, looking at her. He reached into a pocket and took out a cloth bag attached to a thin belt.

"Put the vials in here. There's not much room up there so you would do better to wear them at your side, there isn't enough space to have them at the back, and you'll need to shuffle on your stomach. You don't want to break them. Do you know how to administer them?"

Lena shook her head. She had no medical training, how would she know such a thing? He stood and crossed to a cupboard, pulled out a small tube.

"They look like this inside," he told her. "Slide them out of the holding tubes and you will see two buttons." He held it so she could see. "The first one," he depressed it, "extends the needle".

Lena looked at the long point as it shone in the light. It looked sharp and cruel.

"You insert it, a thigh or arm will do, or the neck if that's quickest, it doesn't really matter as long as it's in a good centimetre."

Lena shuddered. She didn't much like injections, though had given them to the children when necessary, when the drones had brought them from the pharmacy after an online medical examination. This looked much the same, though was slimmer and had no instructions attached.

"Then you just press the button at the end," the nurse was telling her, "just like a normal injection. The chemical will be pushed out, count to five, that will be long enough. Then inject the next clone. We think there are three but we have given you five, just in case".

"In case of what?" wondered Lena. "In case there are more clones? In case I drop one? In case I decide to murder someone extra on my way out?" She kept quiet. He didn't look like he would appreciate her thoughts.

The nurse was standing again, climbing back up. He had no time left, needed to send her on her way. He passed her the screw remover, watched her add it to the cloth bag. He reached out a hand to help her up.

For a moment Lena stood, stared at his hand, did not move. Then she took hold of it, her own small hand swallowed up in the mass of his, let him help her onto the bed. She stood next to him, peering upwards, not at all sure she was strong enough to climb up. Then with no time to think, he hoisted her upwards as easily as he would have lifted a child. She swung her legs into the space and peered forwards. There was a long white tunnel leading away from the entrance shaft. It was lower further on but she had room to sit here, to remain upright. Below her, the nurse was raising the hatch back into place.

"Wait, what are you doing? How will I get out?"

"Don't panic," he told her roughly. "I'm just putting in place, so no one notices. I won't secure it. When you get back, listen. If the room is empty, stamp hard and it will fall down. Then you can get out. Go back to the washroom. You remember the way?"

Lena nodded. Realised he couldn't see her, said, "Yes". Her voice sounded strange, hollow and hoarse.

He paused, lowered the tile again so he could see her. "Good, then go there. At ten o'clock I will come. I will have Max. You can both leave. There will be a car waiting, it will be ordered with a different bar code, make sure you disable the on-board camera. It will take you to the port. Someone will meet you. That's all I know."

He did not tell her to trust him. She had no choice. He did not tell her it would all be fine. He doubted that it would be. He looked up at this woman, saw her exhaustion, her acceptance that she had no options, her determination to find her son. In his mind he wished her well, prayed she would have the strength she needed. He nodded, fixed the tile in place, and left. He did not expect to see her again.

Lena wanted to call after him, to tell him to stay, she couldn't do this. She watched the top of his head go towards the door, then he disappeared from her view. She tied the belt around her waist, hearing the vials jangle against each other. She hoped they were stronger than they looked. Then she leaned forwards into a crouch and began to half crawl, half shuffle, along the narrow vent. She held the map in her left hand. It was folded so that her current position was showing. She needed to go forward past three more vents, then turn right. She felt like a marker in a computer game, wondered if she glowed red.

Crawling was uncomfortable but not difficult. Every so often she lifted her head and looked ahead. She could hear nothing from below, hoped her own shuffling was unheard. She crawled along the narrow space, a fat black cable lying beside her. She tried to not touch it. She arrived at the first vent and peered down. She was looking into a room. There was a nurse in the corner and a bed with a tray next to it. She strained to see around the edge of the vent, to discover who was in the bed. If it was Max, she would abandon her mission in an instant, would find a way to get to him.

It was not. It was an old lady, her white hair flowing over her shoulders, her head resting on a pillow. She was very thin, looked very near death. Lena shuffled on.

The next vent was over a corridor. People passed beneath her, she paused for a moment and watched their heads. Snippets of conversation floated up, none discernible, a general babble of sound. That helped her relax a little, to think that she herself was unlikely to be heard unless she coughed or shouted when above a vent. Whatever the ceiling was made of, it was clearly well insulated, containing both heat and sound. She continued.

At the next vent there was a crossing of routes. She checked the map again, took the fork to the right. Her arms were beginning to tire now and her throat was dry. The tunnels were dusty and dry, uncomfortably hot. She wondered what her uniform must look like now, imagined it was far from the pristine white it had been a few minutes ago. That would be a problem when she came to leave. There was nothing she could do now, so she continued, taking her weight on her arms, shuffling with her legs. An uncoordinated caterpillar.

#

Mel4 was watching her screen closely. She could see that Midra had arrived at the holy place. He had left the car and was moving into position, walking through the clapping public, through the arched doorway and along the aisle. All seemed to be going to plan. She watched the live feed, switching between monitors until he was in his seat at the front. He would be introduced, then would stand and make a speech.

She reached for her keyboard and turned her second screen on. It flashed blue, then she called the island reports back into view. She had made her decision. They could not alter the boy, that was too severe, held too many risks. She thought it was an unreliable method of control, disliked the number of 'failures' her department had been forced to cover up. No, she would not sanction that.

However, her bot had given her three options and the second, the decision to wipe a part of his medium term memory, seemed sensible. He was young, he would have many more years to build new memories. A few gaps wouldn't matter.

She entered the codes, sent her decision. They could do it this morning. He could then be returned to the island, she saw no reason to remove him permanently from his family. Her

179

understanding was that they were planning to leave soon anyway, they could be reunited and go. Then they wouldn't be her problem anymore. It was not as if they were a security threat, they held illegal views, that was all. Mel4 did not agree with the law as it stood, but her job was not to make judgements about that, it was to ensure it was upheld. She finished writing and sent her conclusion. Then she turned back to watch Midra.

#

Lena reached the next vent. She sat up, easing her back, stretching the muscles. This was physically very tough, she wondered if it was going to be possible, she would be tired when she eventually arrived. She peered down, looking for her son. She seemed to be over a cafeteria, she could see heads moving, smell something spicy. It made her feel nauseous. A tendril of hair escaped, tickled her nose. She pushed it back, hooked it into the hairband, noticed her hands were dusty, dry. She wished she had gloves. Wished a lot of things. She checked her map, refolding it so her current position was at the top. The exit shaft, the one near the clones, was now on the same square of paper. She was getting closer. That was good. She had no sense of time but she felt she had been crawling for hours. She checked the vials were still in place, moved them slightly so they didn't knock against her leg, then leaned forwards, continued moving.

#

On the island, John's computer beeped. A message. He opened it. It was sent in code, talked about monitors being fixed, awaiting collection. He smiled, they had located the boy. He checked the time, rubbed his hands together. This was all going to plan. He rose and went to find Den, to tell him to pack, he and Lucy would be leaving on a boat before nightfall. Whatever happened, it would not be safe for them to stay now. Too much was going to change.

The Dance Continues

Lena heaved herself forwards. The white dust had dried her throat, swallowing was an effort. Her arms and shoulders were screaming with tiredness, her back wet with sweat. But she was here, she had arrived at the vent nearest to the clones. She sat up, glad to rest her arms, to stretch her back. Then she leant down and peered through the grill. There was nothing to see, all was white, an empty corridor. She felt into the cloth bag at her side, located the screw remover, looked at it. She had never used one before but had seen them many times. She attached the end to the first screw in the screen, depressed the 'on' button, felt the tiny vibrations as it did its job, watched it turn the screw, hoped the high pitched whirr would not be heard. Hoped many things.

\#

Max was still sleeping. The nurse replaced her computer back on the stand and moved to his side. She checked his vital signs, all good. Then she began to prepare him for the operation, to sterilise and shave his head, to place protective covers across his shoulders. The boy slept on. She worked quickly, they would come for him soon, he needed to be ready.

\#

Mel4 was pacing the room. She held her computer as she walked, eyes glued to the screen, waiting for messages from the bots, using their cameras to scan the crowd, checking for anything unusual.

She saw Midra stand, go to the podium, prepare to make his speech. The camera was behind him, she could see a bald patch in his thin dark hair, his head moving as he spoke. He was clasping the lectern with both hands, his wiry arms protruding from his black sleeves, hair speckling his wrists.

She checked the time. All was to plan. She would be glad when this was over, when her job had returned to the more mundane. Her mind wandered to lunch, she was hungry.

181

On the island, Den was packing a bag. The family didn't have many things, only what they could carry when they arrived. Agnes had given him some food, wrapped in a brown paper package. Lucy was standing next to him, chattering, asking where they were going, when would Lena and Max return, were they going by boat or tube, could she take the models she had made from sticks?

Den told her to leave the models here. He could not answer any of her other questions. His mind was full of worry, organising, asking God to keep his family safe. There was too much that could go wrong, he knew how much he could lose.

The third screw was loose and Lena carefully picked it out of the hole, placed it with the others next to her. She tested the vent, was it secure or would it fall, crashing to the ground when the last screw was removed? It felt firm enough but it was not worth risking. She hooked her nails round the edge, used her other hand to steady the screw remover, to continue unwinding the last thread. It came out easily, was put in the pile with the others.

She began to move the grill. Gently, gently, watching flakes of dust drift downwards, pausing, waiting for shouts or alarms. None came, all was silent. She twisted the grill, allowing it to fit through the gap, placed it next to the screws, waited. Still no sound, no shouts, no alarms. She leant forwards, putting her weight on her arms, lowering her head through the gap, wanting to see what was there. What was waiting for her.

The vent was above a small corridor, a short pathway really. On one side was a room with beds, three patients. They must be the clones. On the other side, beyond a glass wall, were two human guards. They stood, straight backed, legs apart, facing away from the clones, towards a door which she guessed led out of the room, to a general corridor. She stared for a second at their backs, then

182

scanned the rest of the room. There was no one else, no nurses or doctors. At the moment.

Lena pushed herself back up into the space above the vent. She sighed. Now what? The chances of her being able to climb down from the vent, to lower herself onto the floor without causing herself an injury were slim. The chance of doing that unseen by two trained guards was pretty much impossible. If they saw her, they would probably shoot her, restrain her at best. She would then be unable to meet Max. Would her attempt to reach the clones be sufficient? Would John's helpers, this hidden army of star-counters, be willing to remove Max from the hospital? Would they risk their jobs, their anonymity, to help take Max somewhere safe? She didn't know.

There was too much she didn't know. She had heard Nargis say there would be a delayed reaction to the poison she was carrying. How then would injecting the clones cause a diversion? Or was she herself the diversion? Did the planners of this scheme assume she would be caught, that the chaos over her own capture would divert attention away from Max, away from her son, so he could be taken to safety? If she had been told that, she would willingly have complied. But no one had actually told her that. No one had actually told her anything. She felt like a pawn in a great game of chess, moved around by greater minds, useful but expendable.

Memories of Max flooded her mind. She remembered before he was born, the solid lump moving within her, how she would stroke her belly, pray for the baby to be born safely. Even then she loved him, would have given her very life for him. Then watching him when he was tiny, seeing his father's eyes staring at her, her own mouth set in a determined line as he struggled to achieve something. Her body remembered the feel of carrying the toddler Max on her hip; she knew just how he had fitted against her when she carried him around. She had always read him well, even now, as he was changing from boy to man, she often guessed his thoughts, read his mind in a wisp of knowledge carried to her by his expression or tone of voice. He might be physically separate from her but the bond tying them was very strong, almost physical in its intensity. Sometimes she felt overwhelmed by her love for him.

So she was now unwilling to risk being caught. If she knew he would be safe, she would try, she would risk her own safety. But not if that was tantamount to abandoning her son. She had no idea what to do.

In despair, she lowered her head. "God," she prayed, "this is way beyond me. I don't even know how I managed to get into this mess. I'm scared for me and terrified for my son. Could you please just tell me what to do? Should I give up and go back? Should I try to find Max on my own? I am so tired..."

There was no answer, no bolts of lightning, no inner voice telling her what to do. Lena felt utterly alone. She rested her head on her knees and wept.

#

Max was ready. The nurse had been joined by two porter bots. There was no risk of waking the boy, he was heavily sedated. His breathing was regular, heartbeat strong, temperature level. His carer nodded, pleased that he was stable. She didn't stop to wonder who he was, why he was being sent for treatment. It was easier to not think these days, to do your job and comply with instructions. No one had told her that he was special, needed to be watched. The authorities knew that not everyone agreed with their policies. Sometimes it was safer to not announce things, to let people become lost in the system. If the nurse had known the boy was 'high risk', she would never have left. However, she might also have mentioned it to someone. In deciding to avoid the latter, the authorities had not foreseen the former.

She checked the information on the bot's screen. The boy should be gone for about half an hour, perhaps fifty minutes. That was good, she hadn't had her break yet, she could nip down and get a drink, be back in the room by the time they returned him.

She crossed to her computer, sent the updated information, then slipped it into her pocket. She watched as the two bots wheeled the bed from the room, taking it towards the operating room. Then she gathered her things, double checked she had her computer in her pocket and set off for the canteen. The authorities often forgot lower level staff breaks. When there was an emergency they were expected to work straight through. Which was fine in theory but there seemed to be an awful lot of emergencies.

Her mind wandered. Hot chocolate, she thought, that would be nice. They had a new one now, extra thick and creamy but low in sugar, so the sugar tax didn't apply. She could use a break, a chance to switch off for a few minutes. She would be back in the room well before the boy was returned, no one would even know she had left. She began to hum as she walked, she could almost taste that chocolate already.

#

She was beginning to relax when it happened. She had watched Midra make his speech, had kept the volume low, it was hardly going to be earth shattering. Then he had moved to shake the hand of a delegate. There had been a shout, she had spun her camera away, in the direction of the noise, then a bubble of information appeared on her screen, every bot in the holy place sending her information, the bots next to her buzzing as they processed the information, sent her reports to scan and actions to sanction.

She must sanction action. Shoot to kill or tranquillisers? Removal of patient already actioned, car sealed, patient in transit. Did she sanction local hospital or hospital 05? Bots recommended 05, bot in car reported replacement organ likely to be necessary, bleeding under control, heartbeat dropping, fluids administered. Her brain was bursting with information, using the bots advice to decide the best course of action, knowing that her decisions were slow in comparison, that speed mattered.

Mel4 swallowed. Her fingers flew across the keyboard.

'Detain perpetrator, continue medical intervention to stabilise patient, bring him to 05.'

It had happened, Midra had been shot.

She examined the preliminary reports that were being sent from the car. The wound was extensive but unlikely to be fatal. He would need more blood and possibly a transplant, depending on what the bullet had touched. The on-board medical scanners were limited; they would know more when he reached hospital. She decided that 05 was the better option. Then if there was extensive internal damage, if a transplant was necessary, it could be done immediately. She sent the decision, turned back to her other screen.

In the holy place, there was pandemonium. Another man had been shot, probably fatally. One of the human guards had decided to act, to minimise damage. Mel4 suspected he had panicked, shot before he had evaluated the situation. She frowned, now they would have problems finding out who the instigator was, if it was a lone action or part of something bigger. Mel4 told them to try to save the shooter, to take him to the nearest hospital. A team would be waiting for him, they would find out what they could. The guards and bots at the holy place were securing the area, overseeing the safe departure of the delegates.

The bots were still sending her information. She told one to action the safe arrival of Midra to the hospital. The machine whirred, finding vacant rooms, actioning a bed to be prepared, messaging medical staff to leave what they were doing and to be waiting in the correct areas. They cancelled treatment on the boy, that was low priority, and they could use that theatre to treat Midra.

186

They checked security and arranged for further guards to cover the entrances and corridors that the leader would travel down. Within minutes the bots had processed information and made decisions. Mel4 struggled to keep up. This was her job, her fast mind was her main skill, her ability to sanction decisions or cancel them. She was the human element in this, she hoped that was not a hindrance.

#

The message arrived almost instantly to the porter bots wheeling Max. They stopped while they processed the information, then turned, wheeled the bed back to the room. The nurse was just ordering her drink, she was not expecting her patient to return for nearly an hour. She was tired, it was near the end of her shift. She felt her computer vibrate in her pocket, decided to ignore it. She would be back on duty in a few minutes, she would sort out the message then. Sometimes the authorities forgot that nurses weren't machines, couldn't work continually without a break. It was dangerous, irritated her and put the patient's wellbeing at risk. No, whatever it was, it could wait, it was hardly likely to be urgent. She would mention it at the next staff feedback session. This really did happen far too often.

The porter bots wheeled Max into the room. It was empty. Their instructions did not mention being met by a nurse, they had not been alerted that this patient was a high security patient. They were machines. Machines do not worry about possibilities, they respond to instructions. They placed the bed back in the room then continued to their next job, informing the waiting computer that they would be slightly later than expected due to a change in schedule.

Max lay in the bed, his shaved head resting on a pillow, one arm flung from the sheet that tucked him securely in place. He slept on, alone in his room.

#

Lena heard a noise and peered down. She was at the point of abandoning her task, of crawling back to the start and trying to find Max on her own. Before she went, she looked down to see what the noise was. With the grill removed, she could hear quite clearly.

One of the guards was reading a message. He turned to his colleague, said there was a security emergency in zone 26, they should go at once. A high priority patient was arriving; it took precedence over their current position. They both drew their weapons and hurried from the room.

Lena watched them go, their uniformed backs departing through the door. The room was now empty of people. She could hear machines, beeping, whooshing, sucking, but no people. Now what? She knew that the room might not remain empty for long, if this was a chance to inject the clones unseen, then it would be her only one. She was here now, she had come without thinking, driven by tiredness and despair, carried along on by people's will. But she was here. She may as well continue.

She looked at the distance from the hatch to the floor. It was too high. If she jumped she would break a leg, if not worse. There was nothing near to climb onto and she had no rope or anything with her, even if she were strong enough to climb down a rope, which she doubted. She turned onto her stomach and lowered her legs through the hole, aware that if anyone happened to enter the room they would see her before she could react. Then she slid her body, further and further through the gap in the ceiling. The cloth of her tunic snagged on the rough edge, she hoped it wouldn't tear, continued to lower her body. Her weight shifted, pulling her down. There was nothing to hold onto, she grasped the edge of the shaft with her fingers, felt herself slipping, tried to hold her weight on her arms. She was too tired, too unfit, her fingers were not able to keep hold. With a cry, she fell.

She landed heavily, twisting her ankle. When she stood, a bolt of pain shot hotly up her leg, her vision blurred, she fell to the ground. She waited, remembered to breathe, waited for the pain to subside, her head to clear. If anyone arrived now, she would be defenceless, unable to do more than crawl. But no one arrived.

Lena waited until she had recovered enough to try standing again. Cautiously, little by little, she lifted her head. The world did not spin. She did not vomit. She edged upwards, putting her weight on her good leg, crawling towards the nearest bed, using it to haul herself upright. Then she stood there, on one leg, gazing down at the first clone, wondering how long before the guards returned.

Chapter Ten

The Dance Ends

Lena stood very still. She balanced on her good leg, putting no weight on her sprained ankle, looking at the clone. It was a boy, barely any different in age to her boy, to Max. She wondered where Max was now, if he was frightened, whether she would manage to rescue him, whether she would ever see him again. Her eyes filled with tears. She wiped them roughly away. Now was not the time for thinking, she had a job to do, she needed to be quick, before someone arrived.

She reached into the cloth bag at her side and felt the vials. They appeared to have survived her crash landing from the ceiling hatch, seemed to be intact. She withdrew the first one, depressed the end button and the needle shot out. Then she looked again at the clone.

It was surrounded by machines and tubes. The air was warm and filled with the noise of those machines as they breathed, cleaned, fed, the body on the bed. Was it a person? It looked like a boy. Was she about to murder a child?

Until this moment, she had not really considered what her task entailed. She wanted to rescue her son, she had been sent along the electricity ducts to the room of clones, ready to inject them with poison, to stop them functioning. But were they alive? They might be inconvenient to the plans of the people who had sent her, destroying them might improve the life of others, but did that make it right? What actually constituted a human? How human did someone have to be to be counted as a person, to have rights? To have the right to live. She knew the clones were brain dead, could not function at any level without the aid of the machines, had no opinions, no thoughts, no personality. But did that give her the right to destroy them? Were they just a collection of cells, an

190

inconvenient physical form - or were they people? When is a person a person?

Then she thought of her family. Her husband, hounded for his beliefs, her daughter, wrenched from her home, her son, kidnapped and taken for treatment on his brain. They were surely more important, the only thing she should be worrying about. She had no time to think about this.

Feeling uneasy, she inserted the syringe into the neck of the clone. She shuddered as it broke the skin, glided in. Then, turning away, not wanting to see, she pressed the second button, forcing the liquid into its (- his?) body, slowly counting to five as instructed. Trying not to think. She turned back. Nothing looked different. The machines still hummed. The clone lay still, apparently sleeping. Unseen, the poison surged through its body, destroying cells, damaging systems. Each pump of the heart sent it further, deeper, spreading its destruction. But the outside, what people could observe, would remain unaltered for many hours. By tomorrow the first tinge of grey would be visible at the extremities. By evening, the clone would be rotting.

Lena hurried to the second and third clones, repeated her injections. Now she had done one, it seemed easier, she wasted no time injecting the poison. She held the three spent syringes in her hand, not knowing where to put them. If she disposed of them in the room, they might be found, an antidote used, her efforts would be wasted. The needles were sharp, she had nothing to cover them with. She carefully placed them back in the cloth bag; it was the best place for now. One point pierced the material, shining, evil. No, that was a bad plan, if they pierced her she might also die. She took them out, held them where she could see them. Then she looked around the room.

There was a medical trolley next to one of the beds. She swept everything off, the equipment fell to the floor with a crash, she was already wheeling the trolley, pushing it over to below the vent. She put down the syringes, climbed onto the trolley, then reached for them, threw the syringes into the vent, as far away from the entrance as she could. She grasped the edge of the vent, jumped and used her arms to heave herself up. All her muscles groaned at the effort, beads of sweat stood on her neck, she gave a small cry of frustration, kicked her legs. But she managed it. Inch by painful inch, she raised her body upwards, into the hidden shaft above the room.

The cover to the vent lay where she had placed it. She put it back into position, secured it with a screw. There was nothing she could do about the trolley, whoever arrived first would be sure to see it, would look up, see the duct, guess what had happened. But she had too many other things to worry about, she could only achieve so much. The syringes lay where she had thrown them. She picked them up and heaved them further away, deeper into the tunnel beyond the room. Then she lowered herself back into position, began to crawl, began her slow shuffle back the way she had come.

It was much harder going back. Her arms were tired, her head ached. She had also lost the map, had put it down at some point, was now having to remember where to go at each turning. Not that this was difficult, the fine white dust that lined the vents clearly marked her route. It looked as if a giant slug had oozed a trail, sweeping the dust in its wake. She even felt like a slug, dirty and repugnant.

Everything hurt but her ankle cried the loudest, sending heated agony through her whenever she jolted it. She clenched her teeth, determined to return to the entry point, to get back to the washroom, to meet her son. And to drink, to gulp some water into her dry sore throat, to sit and rest her tired limbs. She must keep going, must not give up.

"Don't think, don't think," she told herself, arm over arm, knee after knee, slowly but surely advancing through the shaft.

#

Mel4 was still racing through the reports. Midra had arrived at the hospital, been examined by the medical team. The bullet had pierced a lung, they recommended it should be replaced at once.

A team was sent to prepare the theatre, another to prepare a clone for transplant. The clone needed to be unhooked from most of the machines, rushed to the same operating room as Midra. Everyone was rushing, time was of the essence. Anyone who caused a delay was likely to be penalised, this was not a patient to be relaxed about.

Two young doctors ran to the room where the clones were maintained. The first to arrive, the younger and fitter of the two, saw the mess as soon as he entered. There were instruments in an untidy heap on the floor, a trolley pushed to the middle corridor. He paused, guessed the guards had been in a rush when they left, had run into the trolley, spilling equipment in their panic. He wheeled it out of the way, gave it no more thought and began to prepare the clone.

#

Max was beginning to stir, the sedation wearing off. Opening his eyes was too much effort, but he could hear. Quiet voices were speaking intently, giving instruction. They sounded tense, cross. He wondered why. He was also aware that he was moving. The bed he was in was being rolled across a floor, he could feel a breeze on his head. That was odd. The bed was very soft, comfortable, warm. He would wake up in a minute, he thought, drifting back to sleep.

#

Lena finally reached the hatch where she had entered. She pressed her ear against the grill and listened. Nothing. She peered down, trying to look in each direction. The room seemed to be empty. Using her good leg, she stamped on the grill. It was hard, she couldn't get high enough for there to be sufficient force to knock it from the hole. With a cry of frustration she kicked again. It fell, clattered on to the floor. No one rushed to look. Lena checked, the room was empty, the trolley bed still below the hatch. She lowered herself down, fell with a plop onto the mattress. Her ankle screamed in protest. She almost cried with relief, she was out. But not yet, still a way to go.

Her ankle burned. She needed to sort it before she could go further, it hurt too much to walk. There was a cupboard in the room and she hobbled over to it, checking first that the room door was locked, the glass opaque. There were rolls of bandages, plasters, bottles of liquid, boxes of syringes. Ignoring everything else, she grabbed a bandage, hopped back to the bed. Removing her shoe was agony but she inched it off, then wound the bandage tightly around her ankle, tucking it beneath her heel, giving it some support, some protection. The shoe was now too small to wear on her enlarged foot, so she hopped back to the equipment, found some scissors. They were wonderfully sharp, sliced through the plastic edges of the shoe as if it were cheese. She put the shoe over the bandage. There was a plastic apron in the cupboard, she grabbed it, draped it to cover her dirty uniform, then went to the door.

Opening it slowly, she peered into the corridor. People were passing, lost in their own worlds, hurrying to where they needed to be. No one looked at her, barely seemed to notice her. It seemed impossible that the world should be normal, everyone going about their business, when her world was upside down, everything had changed.

She began to walk. The pain was intense at every step. She willed herself forwards, tried to ignore the pain, the rising nausea.

There was a wheelchair, waiting by the wall in a side corridor. Lena detoured over to it, grasped the handles, used it for support, let it take some of the weight away from her screaming ankle. She switched off the directional motor so that she could push it, guide it to where she wanted to go. It was heavy, her progress was slow but she was advancing, step by painful step, back to the washroom. Her safe haven. The place where she would meet up with Max.

When she arrived at the washroom she abandoned the wheelchair, leaving it against the wall, using the door and walls as her support. She pushed open the door and went inside, looking round expectantly.

It was empty. Lena didn't know if that was because she was too late or too early. She would not allow the thought that they were not coming at all.

There was nothing more she could do, so she went to the sink, turned on the tap. The water was wonderful, filling her mouth, cooling her cheeks. She was still there, bent over the sink, drinking deeply, when the nurse arrived.

He opened the door, saw Lena and came in, leaning against the door to secure it. Arms folded he stood there, watching her for a moment. She didn't hear him, intent on drinking, the water masking the sound of his entry. He took in her pale face, the bandaged ankle, the shaking hands. He allowed himself to smile.

"You made it? Managed to do it?"

His voice was very deep. Lena looked up. Saw he was alone.

"Where is Max?"

"He is safe, we have him. He is sleepy, I will bring him in a chair. Wait in a cubicle, out of sight. We need to get you out of here quickly, as soon as possible."

He paused.

"Well done."

Lena acknowledged the praise, was too tired to do more than nod. He reached up to the hole in the ceiling, passed her the bag, her clothes, her boots. He stood, watching her for a moment longer, as if he would say something else, then changed his mind, turning quickly to the door, leaving Lena alone with her things. She took them into the cubicle, sat, stared at them. Changing was too much effort. She doubted the boots would fit over her damaged ankle anyway. She lowered her head, resting it on her knees and closed her eyes. She may have slept. Time trickled away.

Lena realised she had been waiting for a long time. Her neck was stiff and she raised her head. She was still alone, folded over in her cubicle, dirty, tired and aching. She had no way to check the time, but she wondered what the problem was, the cause for the delay. The nurse had said he was collecting Max. Was he lying? Had he tried to and there had been a problem, had Lena's actions caused some kind of alarm or security alert? Was Max now in more danger than when she had arrived.

She stood, sitting on a toilet would solve nothing. She considered changing into her own clothes, not sure if they would be less noticeable than her dirty uniform when she searched the hospital. She had no plan, only the resolve that she was not leaving without her son, that if the nurse had deceived her, then she must search on her own. For a while she hovered, not moving, groping for a decision, a place to start. She dressed in her own clothes, it seemed a sensible place to start, and she had to start somewhere. She wasn't sure if she had any more resources, could summon the energy necessary to start searching, but she had to do something. Her arms were aching, protested as she pushed them into sleeves. She felt near tears. This wasn't fair. The boots, when she came to them, looked too much of a challenge to even attempt, so she pulled the plastic shoes back onto her feet.

The door being opened disturbed her. She froze, not knowing if someone was using the washroom, or her hiding place had been revealed. She heard her name and rushed out. There was the nurse and a woman. And there was Max, slumped in a wheelchair, pale, bald, alive. She started towards him, then stopped.

"Did they...?" Lena began. Was he hurt, would hugging him cause damage?

"He's unharmed," the nurse reassured her, "he never got as far as surgery. He's just sedated, sleepy. Give him another hour and he'll be awake. He might have a headache but he'll be fine. You need to leave now".

He reached down, picked up Lena's bag and clothes, stowed them under the chair. He put the coat over her shoulders and she realised she was shivering, shaking, was hardly able to stand. The relief at seeing Max was immense. It took her last reserves of energy. She couldn't move, stood for a long moment staring at her son, suspended in time, while the nurse moved around her.

Then she fell forwards, arms around his shoulders, hugging Max to her. She breathed in the smell of him, felt his head hard against her, the warmth of him. Emotions rose hotly inside of her, a great bubble of relief and tears and love that caused a shudder to shake her whole being. He was safe. Her son was safe. She had rescued Max. He moved against her, uncomfortable, and she loosened her grip, eased him back onto the backrest. Her hand rested on his head, feeling the skin, not wanting to move away.

The nurse placed an arm under her elbow and nodded to the woman next to him. She secured a different bar code to Lena's jacket, then opened the door. The group walked quickly, away from the washroom, along the corridor, out through the swishing doors. Lena let herself be led, barely thinking, unable to do more than obey their instructions. Her eyes did not leave her son for a second.

197

There was a car waiting. The nurse led them to it, lifted in Max, helped Lena next to him. He unhooked her bar code, passed it back to the woman. Put Lena's bag on the ledge, where it would obscure the internal camera.

"The car will take you to the port. A boat is waiting. It will take you to the island."

He looked again at the woman and her son. Both almost unconscious. Both brave. Both had achieved more than he would have dreamed was possible. The mother had her arms around her son, holding him close, aware of his warmth, his life. Her eyes shone with tears and her face was streaked with dust and water, drawn into hard lines of tiredness. Yet something about her was stronger than anything he had ever seen before. The almost tangible love of a mother for her child. He wanted to say something, to keep her for longer, to let her know how much he admired her. He was rarely surprised by anyone, but she had astounded him. But he didn't.

He held the bar code under the scanner, shut the door and watched the car drive away.

#

Lena slept most of the journey to the port. When she woke she reached again for Max and held him close, tight, as if he might disappear. She watched the scenery as it glided past the window, trees, hedges, buildings, roads stretching to the horizon.

The port was in the centre of a town, down a narrow street, past people walking, carrying on with their lives. Her time in the hospital was becoming dreamlike, it was incompatible with the normality of the life she could see through the window. The car slowed as it neared the water.

As soon as the car stopped, the door was opened from the outside and a man, who she did not recognise but who called her Lena, helped her to carry the dozing Max, took her to a fishing boat. She sat on deck, shivering in the cold, spray dampening her hair, the wind blowing away her worries, reminding her that she was alive, she had survived. The motor started, and they eased away from the dock. No one had spoken, other than instructions as to where she should sit, where to stow her bag. It had all happened automatically, and Lena again had a sense of being a small part in a big machine. Though if she was honest, she was so tired that decisions were probably beyond her, she was happy to be guided. Max was beginning to wake. Every so often he would look at her with bleary eyes, smile, then drift away again.

The boat crossed the narrow strip of sea to the island. John and Agnes were waiting, with Den and Lucy. They were huddled on the jetty, collars turned up against the wind. Den leaped on to the boat, hugged her, wordless, tears running down his cheeks. No attempt to control his racing emotions, no desire to appear manly, strong. He had thought he had lost her. He loved this woman, with her corners and frowns and doubts. She was part of him. He held her close, breathing in her tangled hair, smelling the dust on her. She pulled away, needing to breathe, smiled up at him.

John told them to hurry, the boat needed to leave. They passed bags to the family, Agnes handing them a parcel, telling them there were sandwiches. Lena was shaking, the cold seeping through her thin jacket and into her bones. John noticed, gave her his own coat, told her to wear it, to stay safe. Then he and Agnes stepped back, waving arms in big arcs as the boat moved away, the motor sending black smoke into the air, bouncing across the waves. They watched the family leave, grow smaller and ever more distant. They were glad they were safe, were looking forward to a return to normality. Yet Agnes knew that a part of her was leaving with them, she would never forget this little family.

Beside her, John waved in silence. His plans were almost complete, the family would be an obstacle now, it was better that they left, hurried to safety before they started asking questions. They had not been as compliant as he had hoped, but it didn't matter now, the result had been achieved.

Lucy was frightened in the boat, thought they might sink. Lena was beyond being frightened of anything. She held her daughter on her lap, letting her body warm her, whispering songs into her hair. She liked the feel of the boat as it rose and fell with the waves, riding over the powerful ocean, carried along with no attempt to resist. Den held Max, took him to the edge when he needed to vomit, wound a scarf over his bare head to keep him warm. He was fully awake now but aware only of the immediate, the cold, the sickness, his headache. He had no idea what was happening, where they were going or why. Nor did he care. Talking would come later.

They arrived on the French shore. More people were waiting, more friends who they had never met. Lena wondered if they were stars, if John had counted them.

They were bundled into a car, driven through towns and cities until they reached Paris. More people, old buildings, many cars. Then they were left at the station, a stranger's bar code was used to pay the fare. They sat on the platform, waiting for the tube train that would take them onwards. At their feet were bags, donated by more unknown friends, food, clothes, provisions for the journey. Lena wondered how big this network of people was, just how many people John controlled. She leant against Den, happy for him to be the strong one, to be able to let go for a while. She thought again about her journey, her mission. She wondered if it was enough, if she could now be counted amongst the stars. Worried that it might not be, that there was something more, something she had missed. She was still tired, groping with the thought, trying to sort it out in her mind.

Den felt her tension, held her close. "What's the matter little one? We're safe now, we've left England. No one will care about us now."

"Den, I've been thinking, about the stars that John counts, the Jews and Muslims. I understand how he includes them, they are mostly born into their faiths, they practice their religions, follow rituals, believe their holy books…. But what about the Christians? How does God decide if they are good enough, have done enough to qualify as stars? How can they be sure they will be counted?"

Den moved slightly so he could look at her. He saw the clouds in her eyes, the worry that loomed there in spite of how far they had come.

"But Lena," he said, "no one can do enough. That's the point of Christianity. You cannot earn the right to be a star. A star is an honorary son of Abraham, an *adopted* son if you like. Adopted by God. None of us is good enough for that, that's the point."

Lena frowned. What then, was the point? Had all her efforts been in vain? Would she still be rejected?

Den continued, "When you were in the hospital, saving Max, it was difficult wasn't it?"

Lena nodded, remembering the pain in her ankle, the fear, the never ending dusty vents.

"But you didn't do it so he would owe you something, so you would have a hold over Max, to control him. And you wouldn't want him to go back into the hospital, to do it again, for himself would you? To go back and inject the clones, to risk capture, so he could say that he had done it for himself?"

"No," she frowned, "of course not. I don't think he could have done it anyway". She thought of the ducts, the long crawl, the drop from the ceiling. "He isn't big enough to have done it," she said, feeling slightly irritated with Den now. It was a silly question. She had achieved what she had for her child, why would she want him to go back and do what was unnecessary? "I had to do it, so the watchers would help me. I did it because I love him, I wanted to save him. I didn't want them to change him, I wanted him to be himself, to be safe."

Den moved his hand, stroked her hair. Explained, "Well, that's how it is with God. He's done all the hard work, He just wanted to save us. We just have to let Him."

Lena looked at him, her eyes bright with tears. She so wanted that to be true, she wanted to belong. Was it really just a case of accepting?

He bent down, kissed her nose. "You will always be the brightest star in my eyes," he whispered as the train slid towards the platform, hovering over the rails, the electromagnets bringing it to a perfect stop.

Max glanced at his parents, then looked away quickly. They could be so embarrassing sometimes. He stared at the train through the thick glass seal. The vacuum enclosed casing retracted, unsealing the train, giving access to the platform. The train doors swooshed open and he went to help Lucy lift her bags. She glanced at his bald head, grinned, said nothing.

The train was large, tubular in shape with thick walls to keep the air inside. The tubes it travelled along were vacuums, the electromagnets allowing great speeds as it hovered above the rails. The family climbed aboard. They were leaving, going to a new life in Asia, being guided by the stars to a place they could be free. It had been a hard journey, they had nearly been stopped many times, but they were on their way now. And they were together, they had survived.

They did not see the newsfeed on the screen behind them. It was very large, projected images of a reporter giving sombre news, announcing the death of Midra. The leader of the Global Council was dead.

Nor did they see the pictures of the man who was to be his successor, the newest member of the Global Council, the person who would decide how England was to be ruled. A young man, very tall. It was his eyebrows that you noticed first, they rose upwards, giving him the appearance of an owl. A great horned owl.

He was the last puppet in the dance.

The End

Also by Anne E. Thompson

Hidden Faces
Invisible Jane
JOANNA

Clara Oakes (due 2018)

See anneethompson.com for details

Read on for an extract from JOANNA

Chapter One

My Story

I first saw them on the bus. They got on after me, the mother helping the toddler up the big step, holding the baby on her hip while she juggled change, paid the driver. I wondered why she hadn't got her money ready, been prepared so we didn't all have to wait. I watched as she swung her way to a seat, leaning against the post for support, heaving the toddler onto the chair by his shoulder.

Then they sat, a happy family unit, the boy chattering in his high pitched voice, the mother barely listening, watching the town speed past the window, smiling every so often so he knew he had her attention. Knew he was loved. Cared for. They had everything I didn't have but I didn't hate them. That would have involved feelings and I tended to not be bothered by those. No, I just watched, knew that those children had all the things, all the mothering, that had passed me by. Knew they were happy. Decided to change things a little. Even up the score, make society a little fairer, more equal.

Following them was easy. The mother made a great deal about collecting up their bags, warning the boy that theirs was the next stop. She grasped the baby in one hand, bus pole in the other and stood, swaying as we lurched from side to side. She let the boy press the bell button, his chubby fingers reaching up. Almost too high for him. Old ladies in the adjoining seats smiled. Such a cosy scene, a little family returning from a trip to the town. They waited until the bus had swung into the stop, was stationary, before they made their way to the door. I was already standing, waiting behind them. The mother glanced behind and I twisted my mouth into a smile, showed my teeth to the boy who hid his face in his mother's jeans, pressing against her as if scared. That was rude. Nothing to be frightened of. Not yet.

The family jumped from the bus and I stepped down. As the bus left I turned away, walked the opposite direction from the family. In case someone was watching, noticing, would remember later. Not that that was a possibility but it didn't do to take chances. I strode to the corner, turned it, then made as if I had forgotten something. Searched pockets, glanced at watch, then turned and hurried back. The family was still in sight, further down the road but not too far. She had spent time unfolding the buggy, securing the baby, arranging her shopping. All the time in the world.

I walked behind, gazing into shop windows, keeping a distance between us. They left the main street and began to walk along a road lined with houses, smart semi-detached homes with neat square gardens. Some had extended; built ugly extra bedrooms that loomed above the house, changing the face, destroying the symmetry. There were some smaller houses stuffed by greedy builders into empty plots, a short terrace in red brick. It was just after this the family stopped.

The mother scrabbled in her bag, retrieved her key. The boy had skipped down the path, was standing by the door. The mother began to follow but I was already turning away. I would remember the house, could come back later, when it was dark. I would only do it if it was easy, if there was no risk. If she was foolish enough to leave the back door unlocked. No point in going to any effort, it wasn't as if they meant anything to me. There would be easier options if it didn't work out. But I thought it probably would. There was something casual about her, about the way she looked so relaxed, unfussy. I thought locking the back door would be low on her priorities until she went to bed herself. People were so complacent, assumed the world was made up of clones of themselves. Which was convenient, often worked to my advantage. As I walked back, towards the bus stop, I realised I was smiling.

***

JOANNA is now available from Amazon and all good bookshops.

18850421R00127

Printed in Poland
by Amazon Fulfillment
Poland Sp. z o.o., Wrocław